Sports Illustrated KIDS

GRAPHIC NOVELS

▼▼ STONE ARCH BOOKS
a capstone imprint

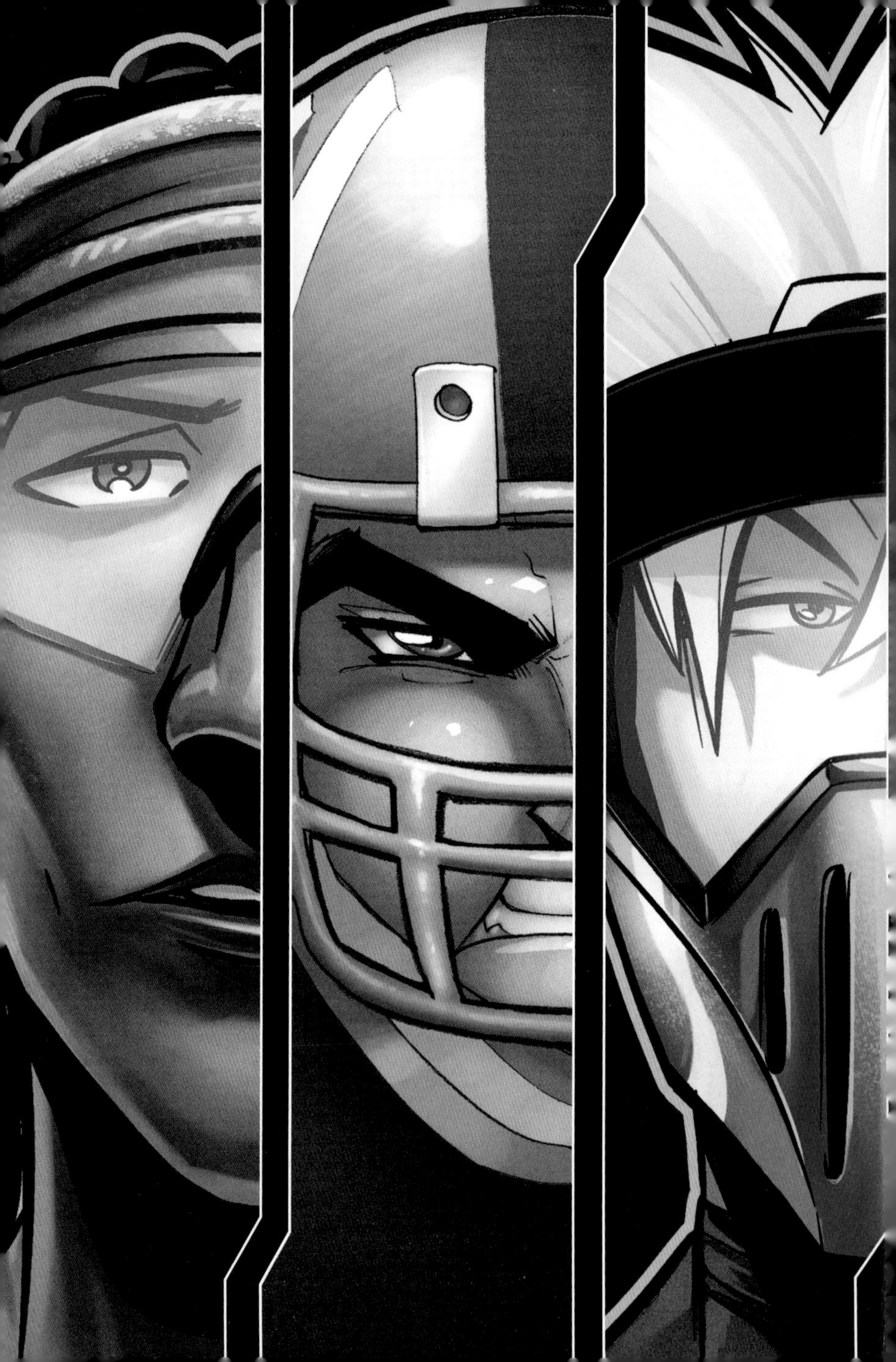

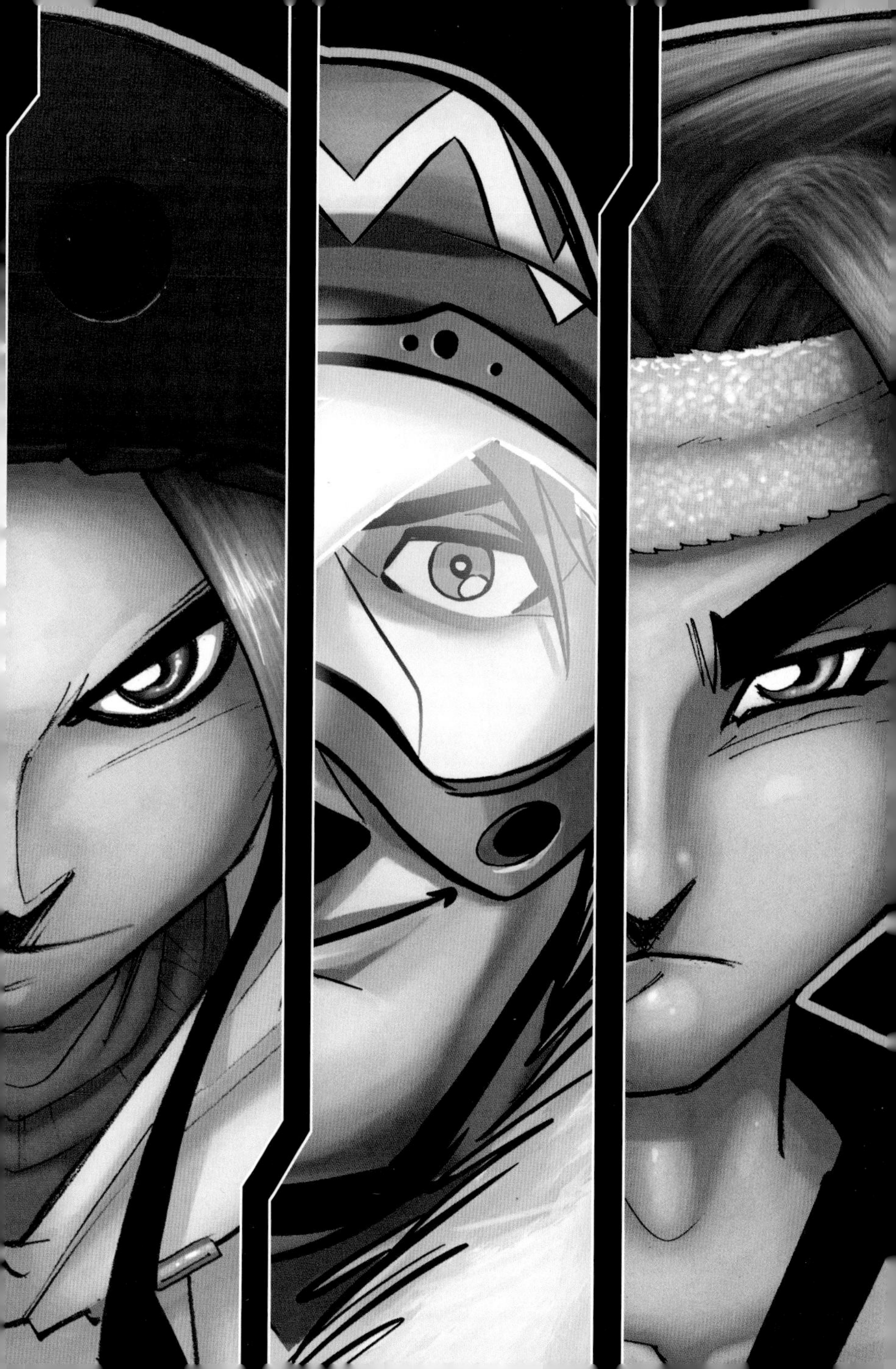

UP NEXT ›››

on Sports Illustrated KIDS

:02 SPORTS ZONE SPECIAL REPORT

:04 FEATURE PRESENTATION:

SKATEBOARD BREAKDOWN

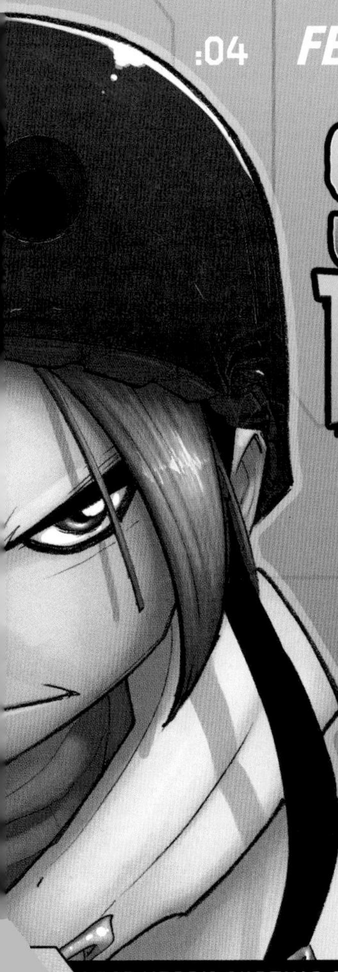

FOLLOWED BY:

:50 SPORTS ZONE POSTGAME RECAP

:51 SPORTS ZONE POSTGAME EXTRA

:52 SI KIDS INFO CENTER

LAST YEAR'S SKATING CHAMP, BING HAWTIN, ARRIVES TODAY SIK TICKER

TEEN SKATER STRUGGLES TO COPE WITH TRAGIC LOSS OF HEROIC OLDER BROTHER

TYSON TAGGART

STATS:
AGE: 14
NICKNAME: TY

BIO: Ty's older brother, Nick, recently died in service of our country. Ever since then, Ty has been struggling to stay balanced — on his board, *and* in his life. He's skating recklessly, making fans wonder if Ty still has what it takes. But this weekend, we'll find out — Ty will be put to the test against the best of the best, the reigning skatepark champ, Bing Hawtin.

EDWIN PEREZ

AGE: 21 **JOB:** SOLDIER

BIO: Edwin was Nick Taggart's best buddy in the Armed Forces. He's come to town to visit Ty, hoping to steer the struggling skater back on the right track.

BLZ vs BHS	**3·1**
TGR vs ROR	**33·32**
EAG vs BAN	**14·7**
SPA vs WLD	**4·3**
BAN vs LIG	**21·15**
ROR vs LIG	**4·3**
BLZ vs BHS	**3·1**

JENNY STEIN

AGE: 15

BIO: Ty's best friend and most loyal supporter. If Ty's competing in a skating contest, Jenny will be cheering him on from the sidelines.

STEIN

BRENDA TAGGART

AGE: 36

BIO: Ms. Taggart is Ty's supportive, strict mother. She takes no bull from Ty, and she keeps him on track and focused on what's important.

MS. TAGGART

JILLY SPEARS

AGE: 19 **JOB:** SKATEPARK OWNER

BIO: Jilly Spears is a patron of the skateboarding art. She regularly hosts competitions and charity drives at her skatepark.

SPEARS

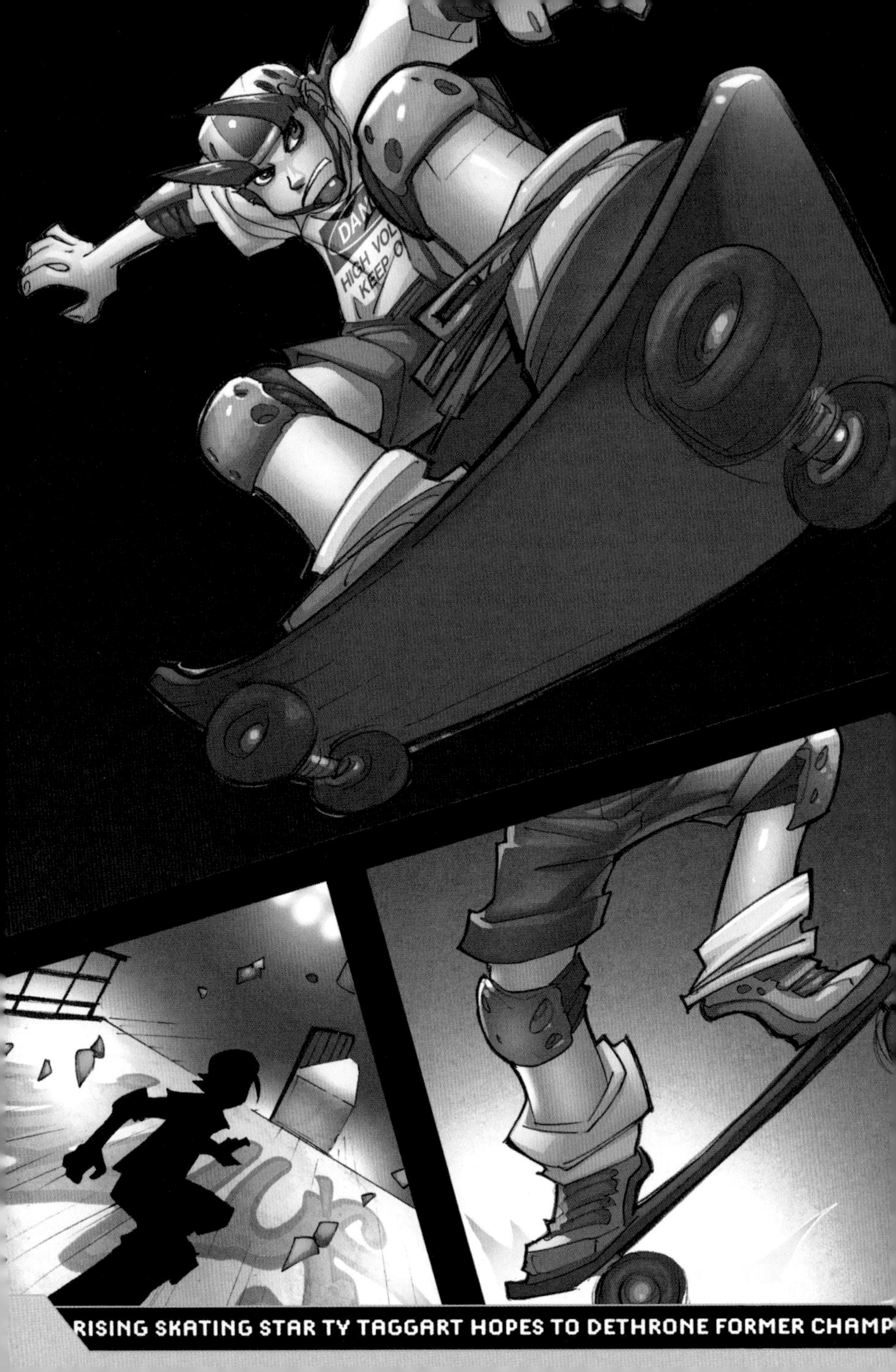
RISING SKATING STAR TY TAGGART HOPES TO DETHRONE FORMER CHAMP

Sports Illustrated KIDS

PRESENTS

SKATEBOARD BREAKDOWN

A PRODUCTION OF

STONE ARCH BOOKS
a capstone imprint

written by Eric Fein
illustrated by Gerardo Sandoval
colored by Benny Fuentes

designed and directed by Bob Lentz
edited by Sean Tulien
creative direction by Heather Kindseth
editorial direction by Michael Dahl

Sports Illustrated KIDS *Skateboard Breakdown* is published by Stone Arch Books, 151 Good Counsel Drive, P.O. Box 669, Mankato, Minnesota 56002.
www.capstonepub.com

Summary: Ty Taggart has always loved skating. But ever since his older brother, Nick, died in combat, Ty has been off his game. He skates recklessly and has lost all interest in the local skating tournament. But when Nick's best friend, Edwin, pays him a visit, Ty is able to reign in his anger and realize his true skating potential. In the finals, everyone is dazzled by Ty's slick, flashy tricks — until he wipes out and breaks his board. Ty will have to pick up the pieces and reassemble his board overnight if he hopes to prevail.

Cataloging-in-Publication Data is available at the Library of Congress website.

ISBN: 978-1-4342-2011-0 (library binding)
ISBN: 978-1-4342-2785-0 (paperback)

Printed in the United States of America in Stevens Point, Wisconsin.
032010 005741WZF10

R-SKATER BING HAWTIN, IN THIS YEAR'S SKATEPARK SHOWDOWN SIK TICKER

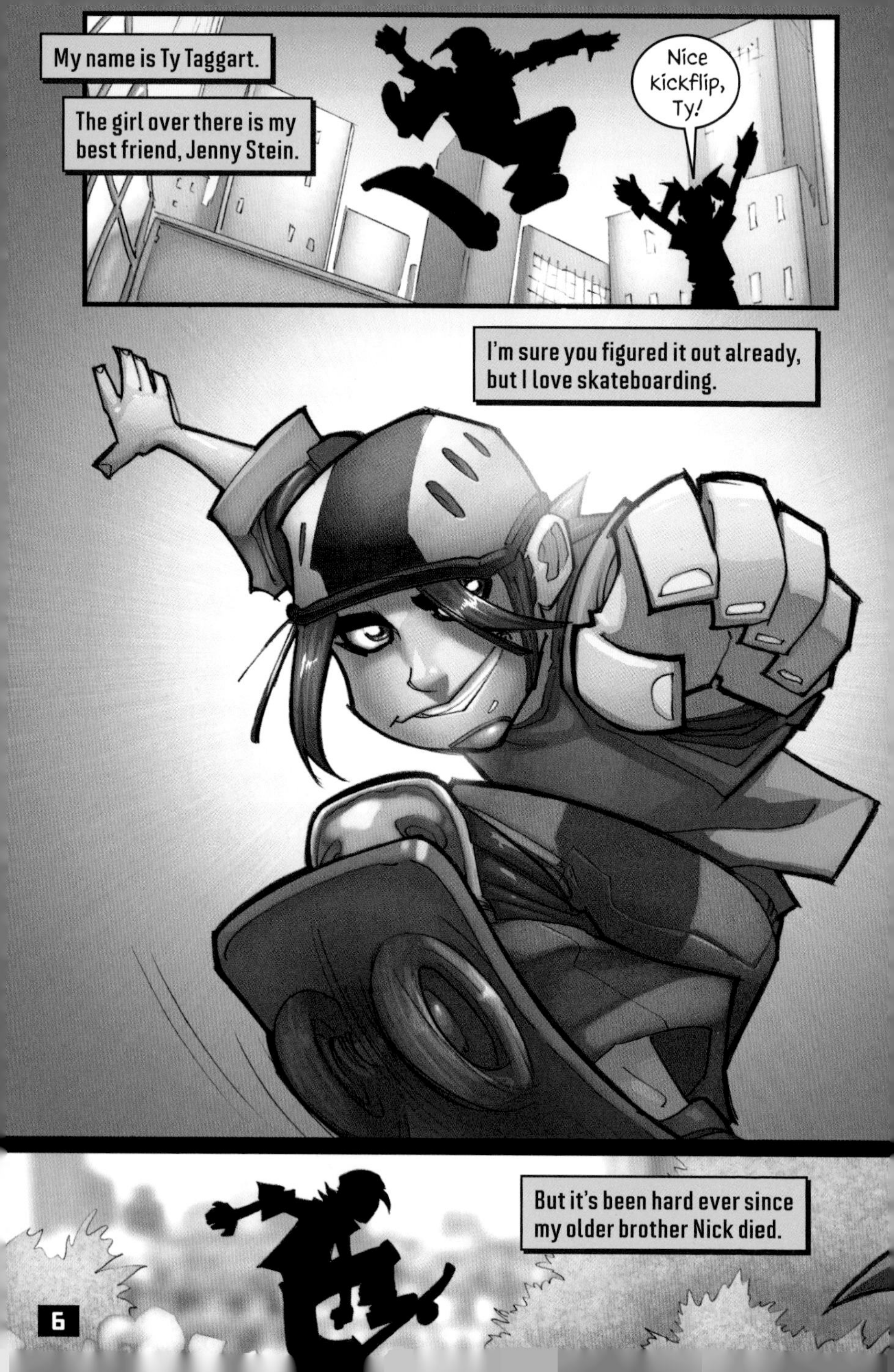
My name is Ty Taggart.
The girl over there is my best friend, Jenny Stein.
Nice kickflip, Ty!
I'm sure you figured it out already, but I love skateboarding.
But it's been hard ever since my older brother Nick died.

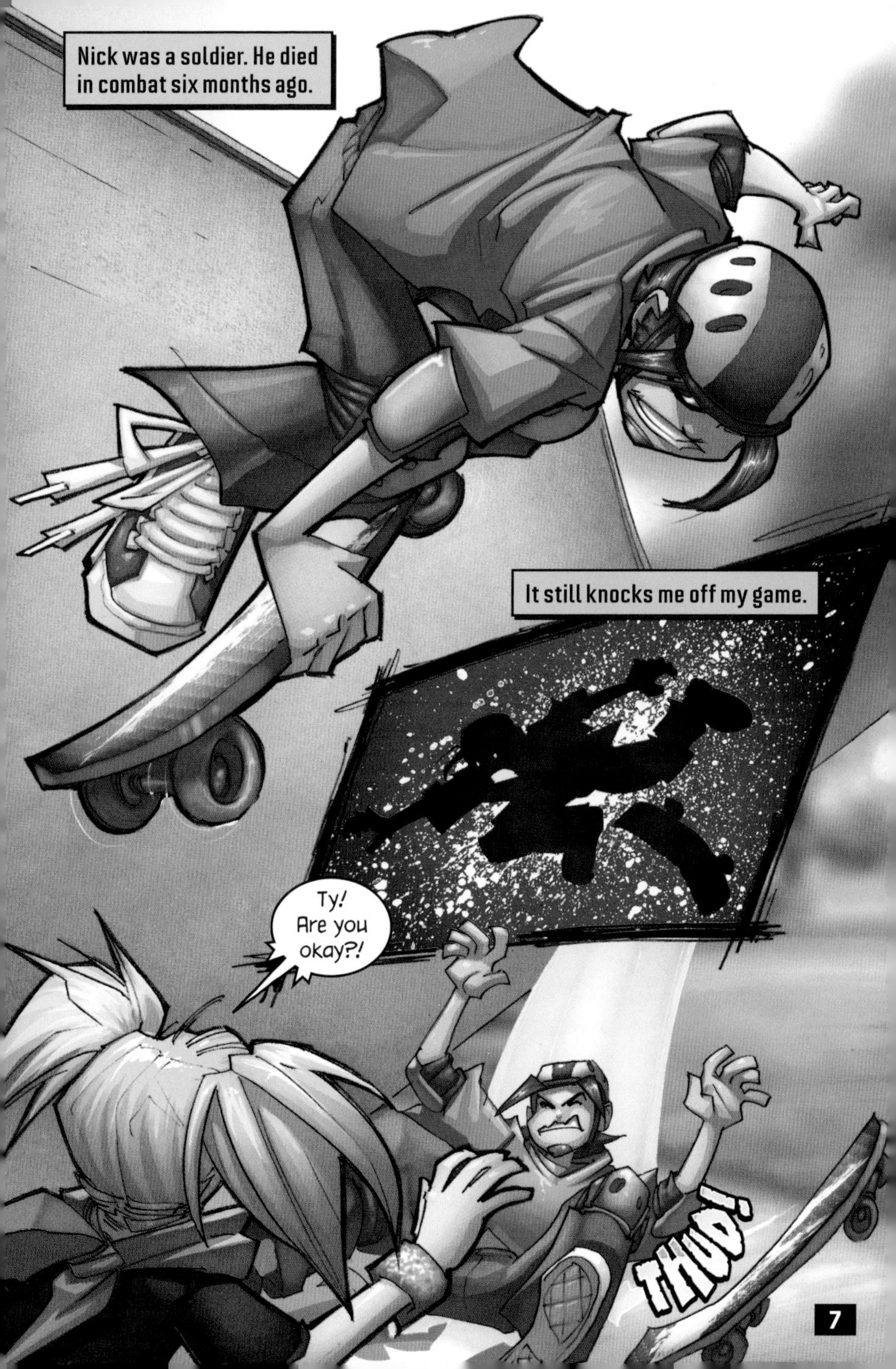
Nick was a soldier. He died in combat six months ago.
It still knocks me off my game.
Ty! Are you okay?!
THUD!

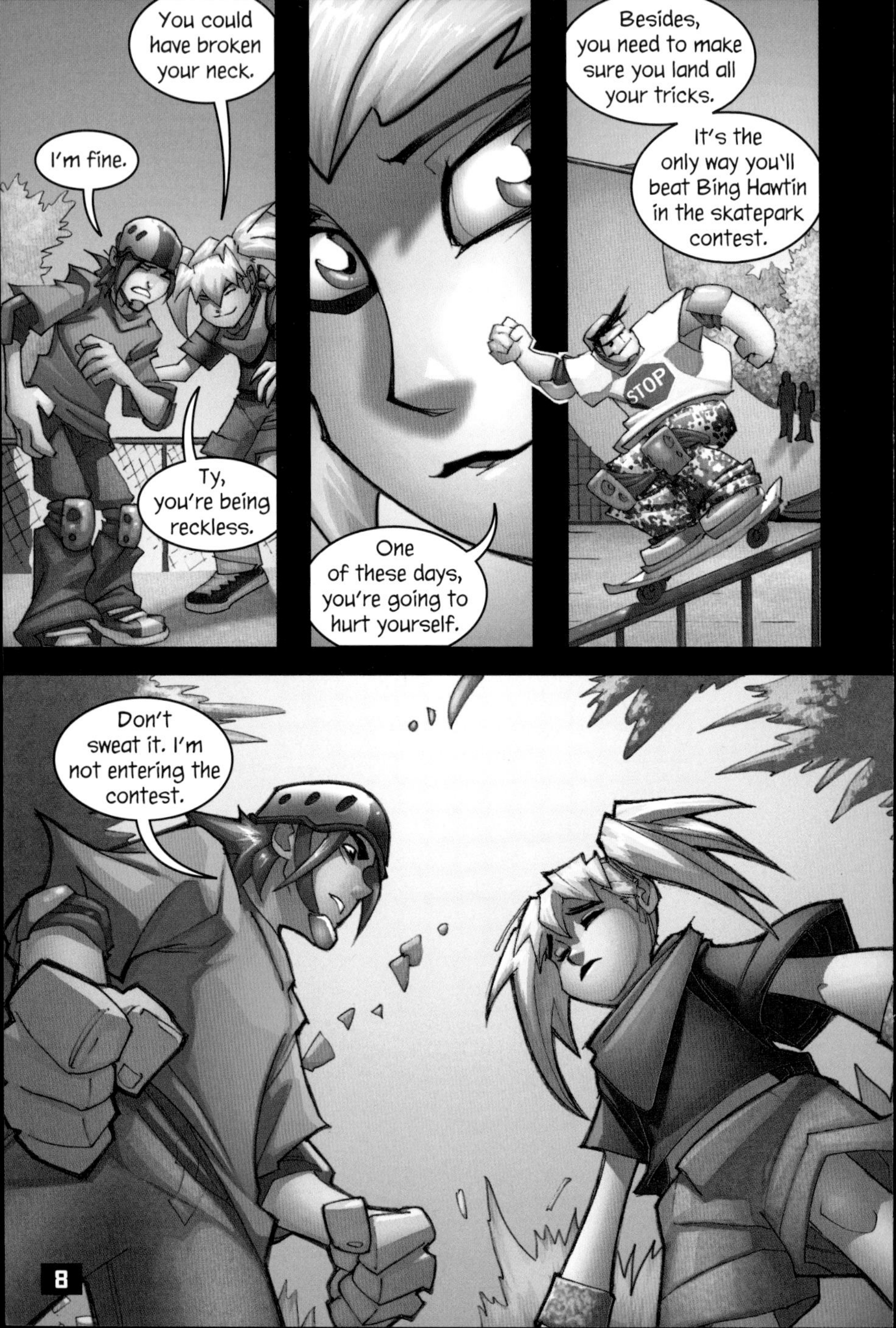
I'm fine.
You could have broken your neck.
Ty, you're being reckless.
One of these days, you're going to hurt yourself.
Besides, you need to make sure you land all your tricks.
It's the only way you'll beat Bing Hawtin in the skatepark contest.
STOP
Don't sweat it. I'm not entering the contest.

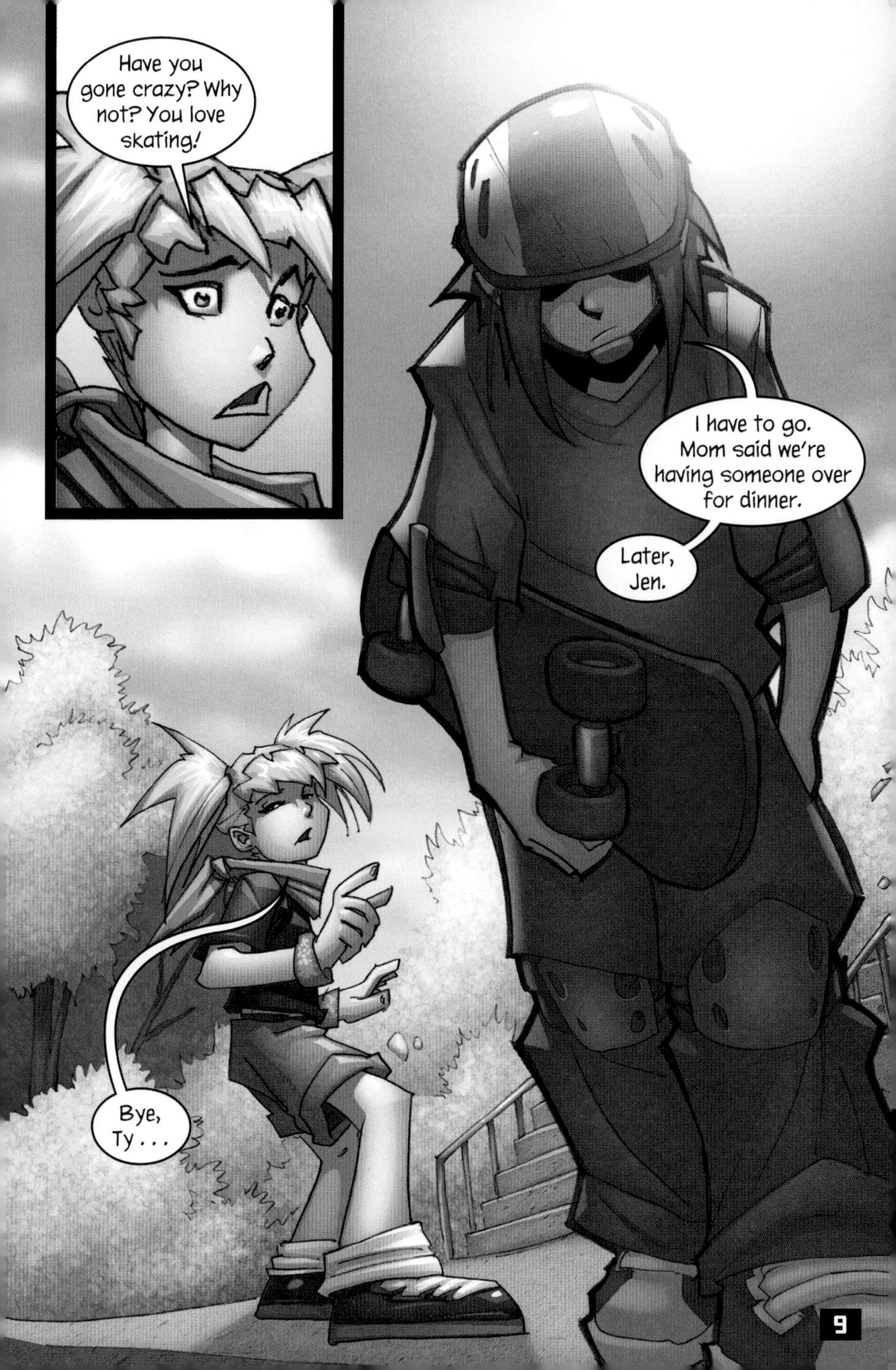
Have you gone crazy? Why not? You love skating!
I have to go. Mom said we're having someone over for dinner.
Later, Jen.
Bye, Ty . . .

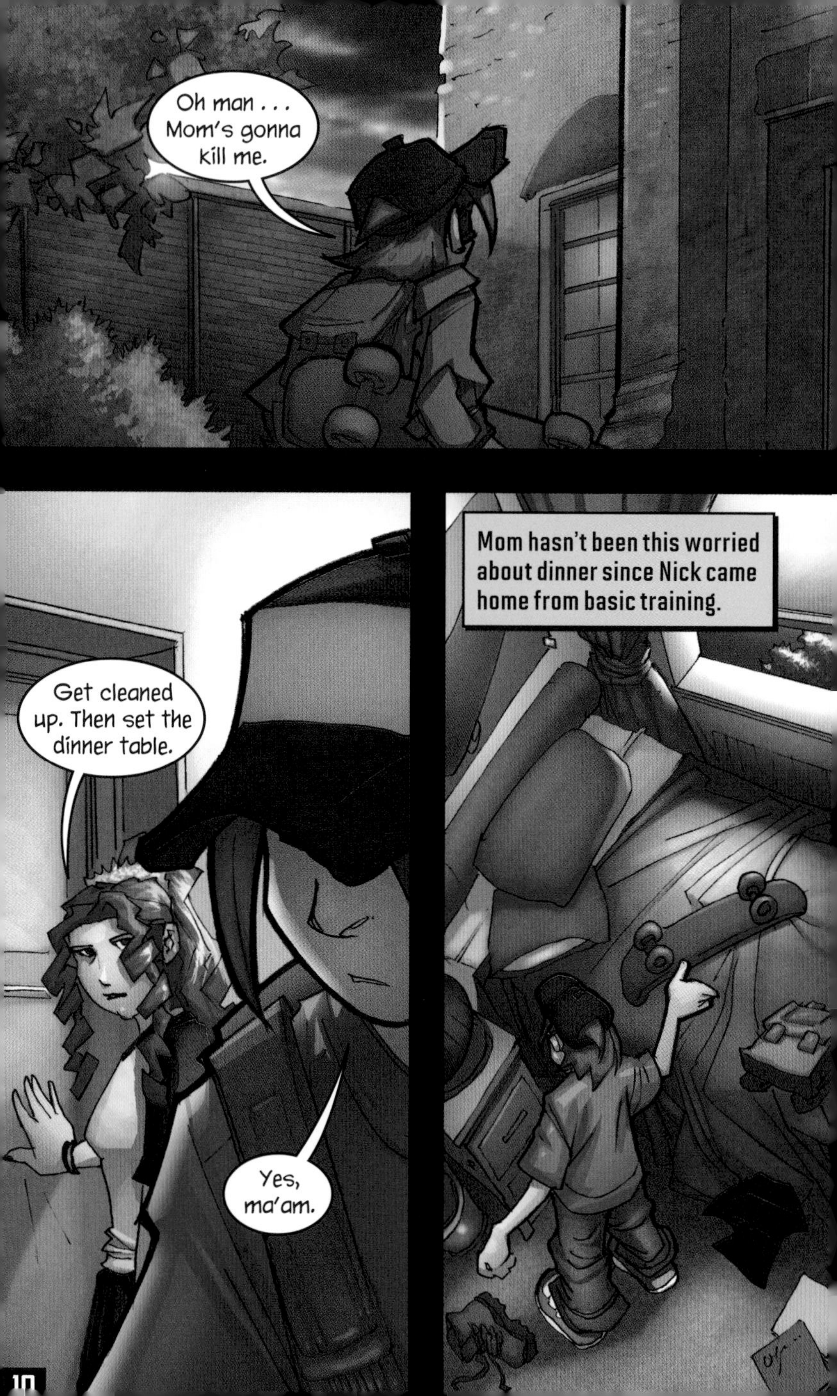
Oh man . . . Mom's gonna kill me.
Get cleaned up. Then set the dinner table.
Yes, ma'am.
Mom hasn't been this worried about dinner since Nick came home from basic training.

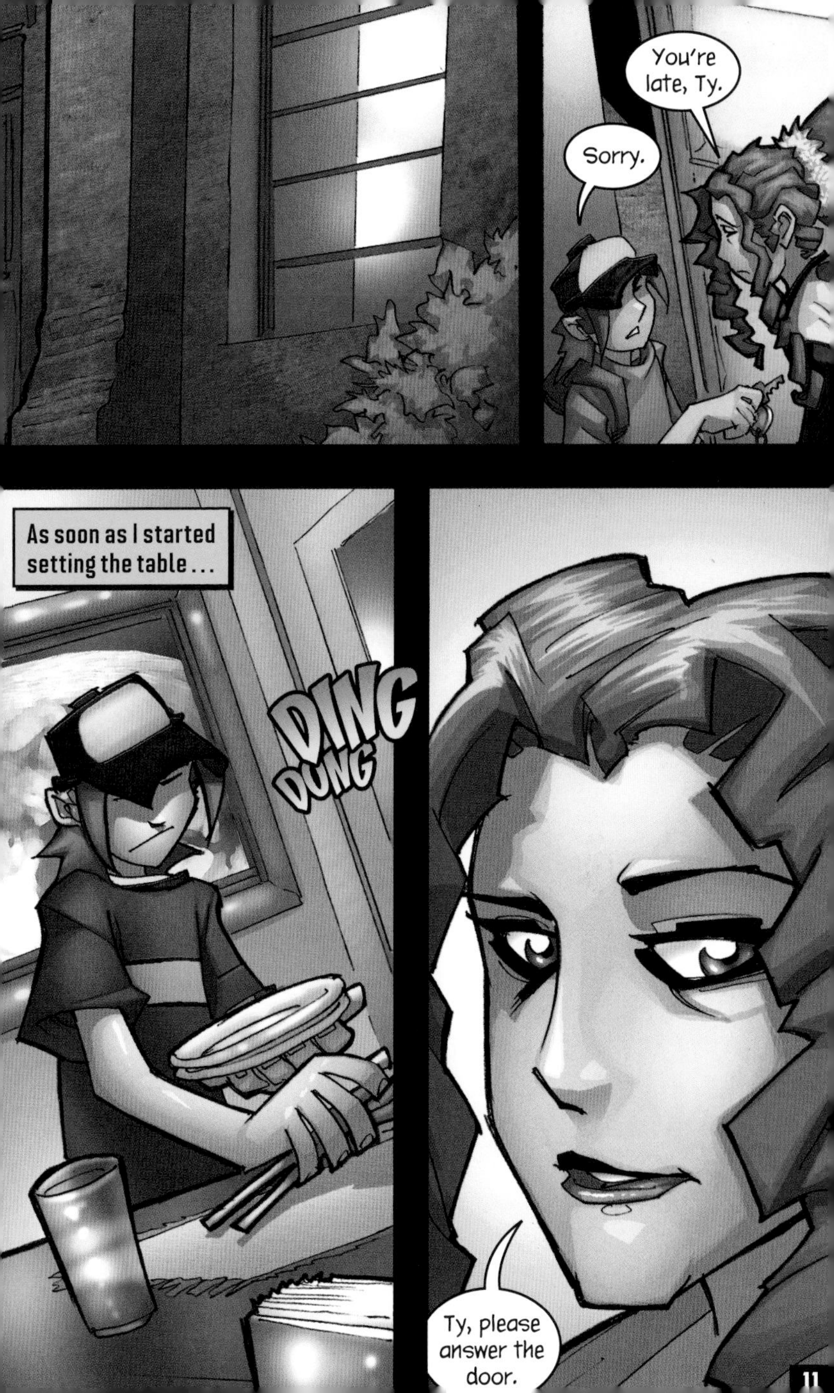
You're late, Ty.
Sorry.
As soon as I started setting the table . . .
DING DUNG
Ty, please answer the door.

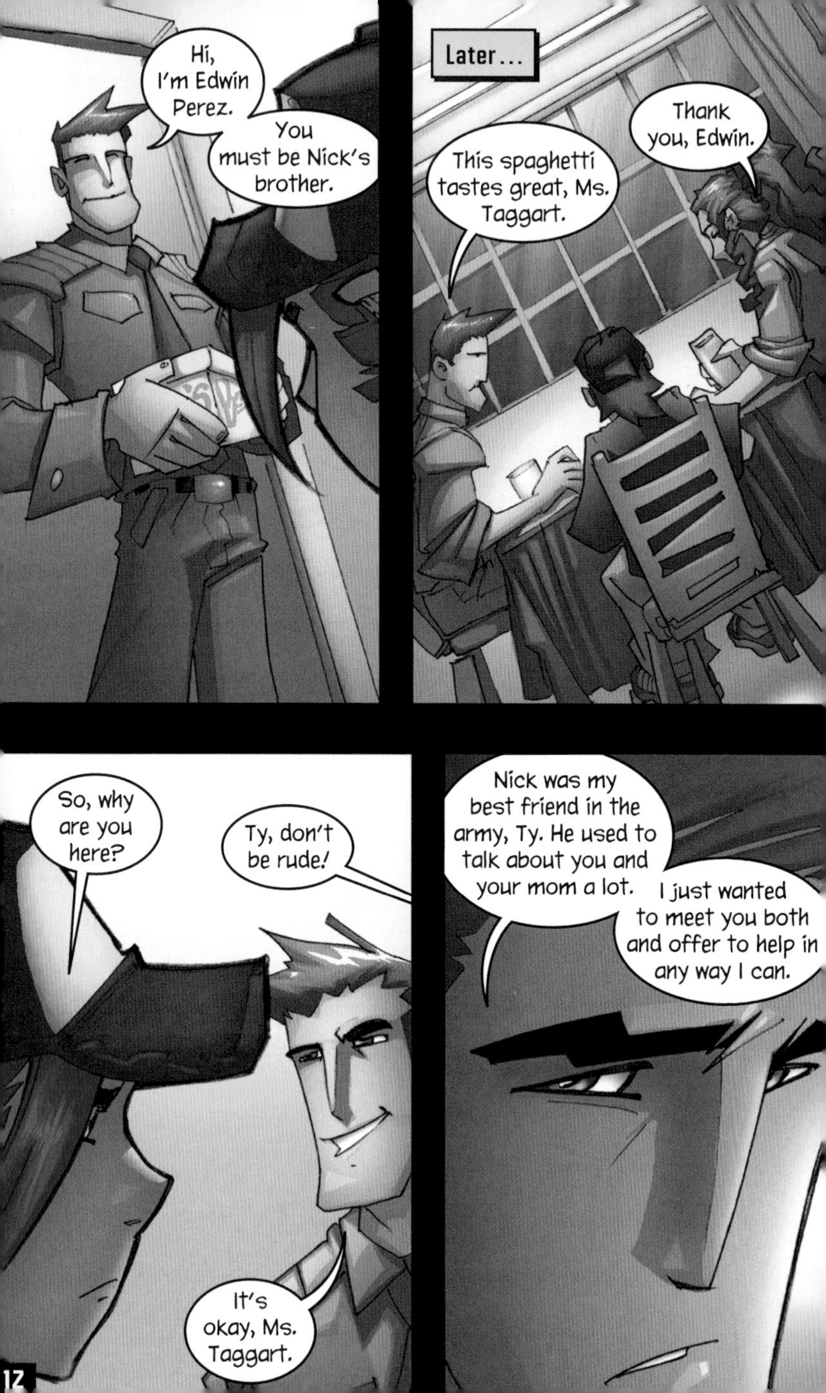
Hi, I'm Edwin Perez.
You must be Nick's brother.
Later...
This spaghetti tastes great, Ms. Taggart.
Thank you, Edwin.
So, why are you here?
Ty, don't be rude!
It's okay, Ms. Taggart.
Nick was my best friend in the army, Ty. He used to talk about you and your mom a lot.
I just wanted to meet you both and offer to help in any way I can.

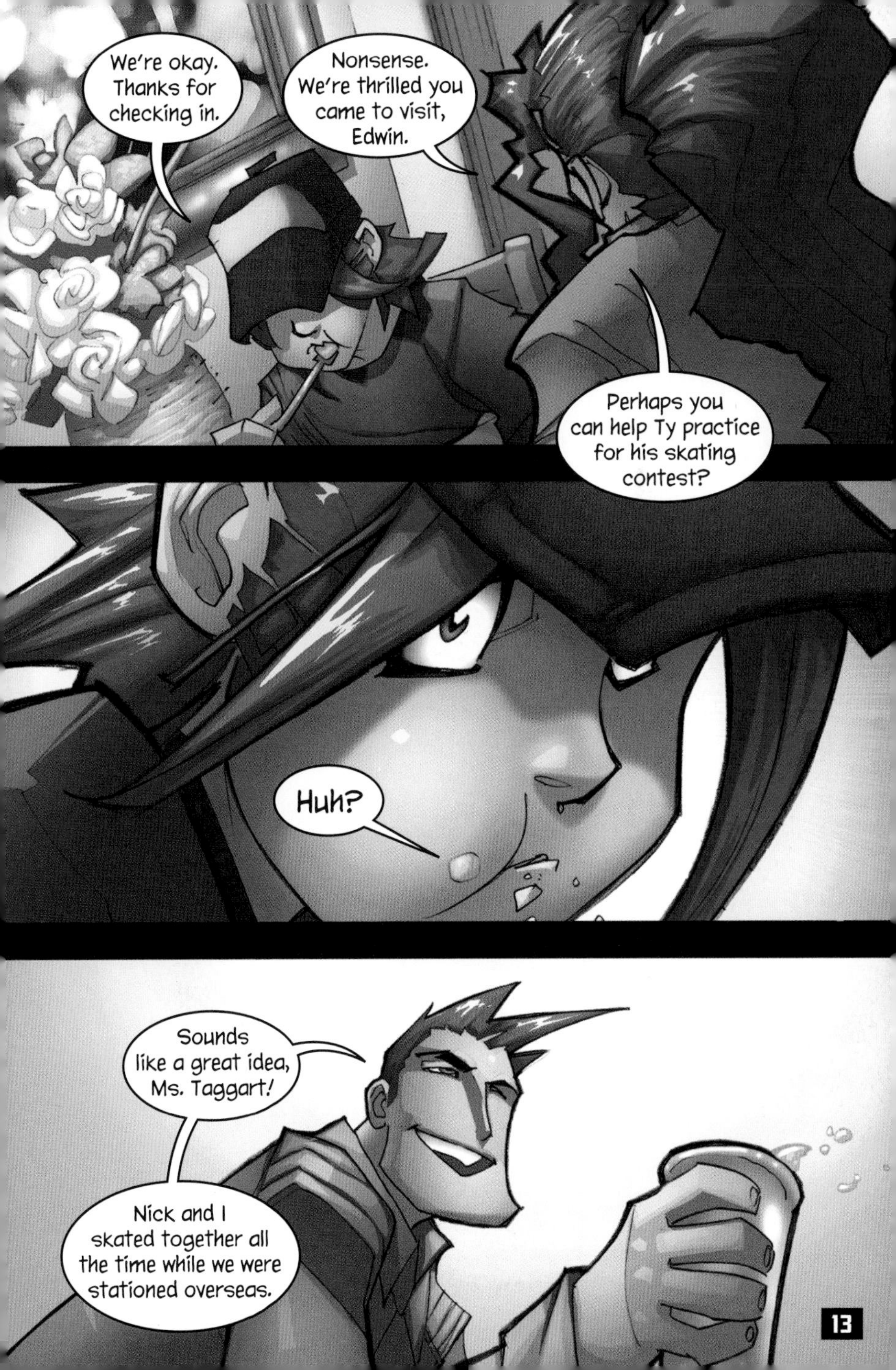
We're okay. Thanks for checking in.
Nonsense. We're thrilled you came to visit, Edwin.
Perhaps you can help Ty practice for his skating contest?
Huh?
Sounds like a great idea, Ms. Taggart!
Nick and I skated together all the time while we were stationed overseas.

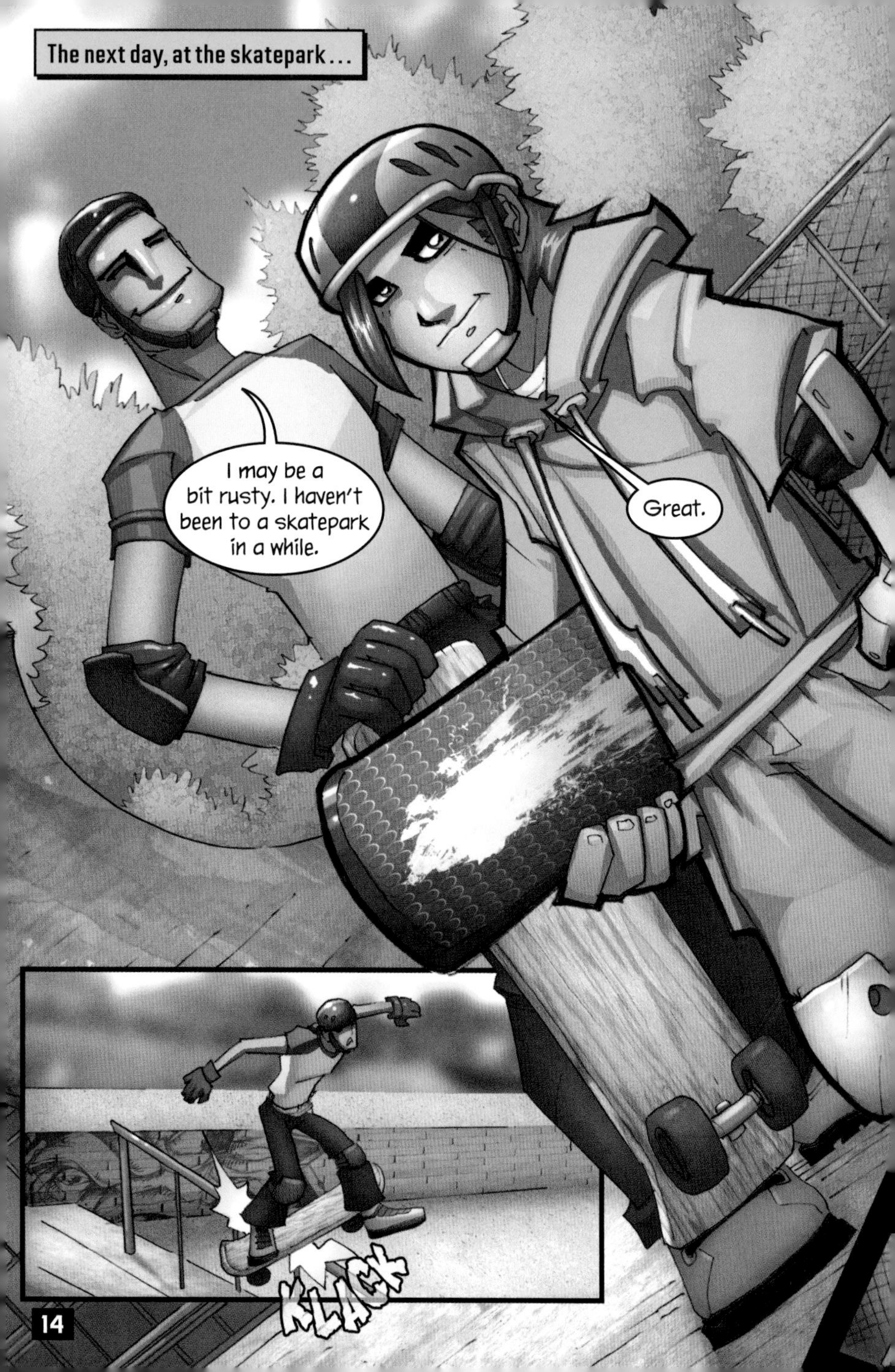
The next day, at the skatepark . . .
I may be a bit rusty. I haven't been to a skatepark in a while.
Great.
KLACK

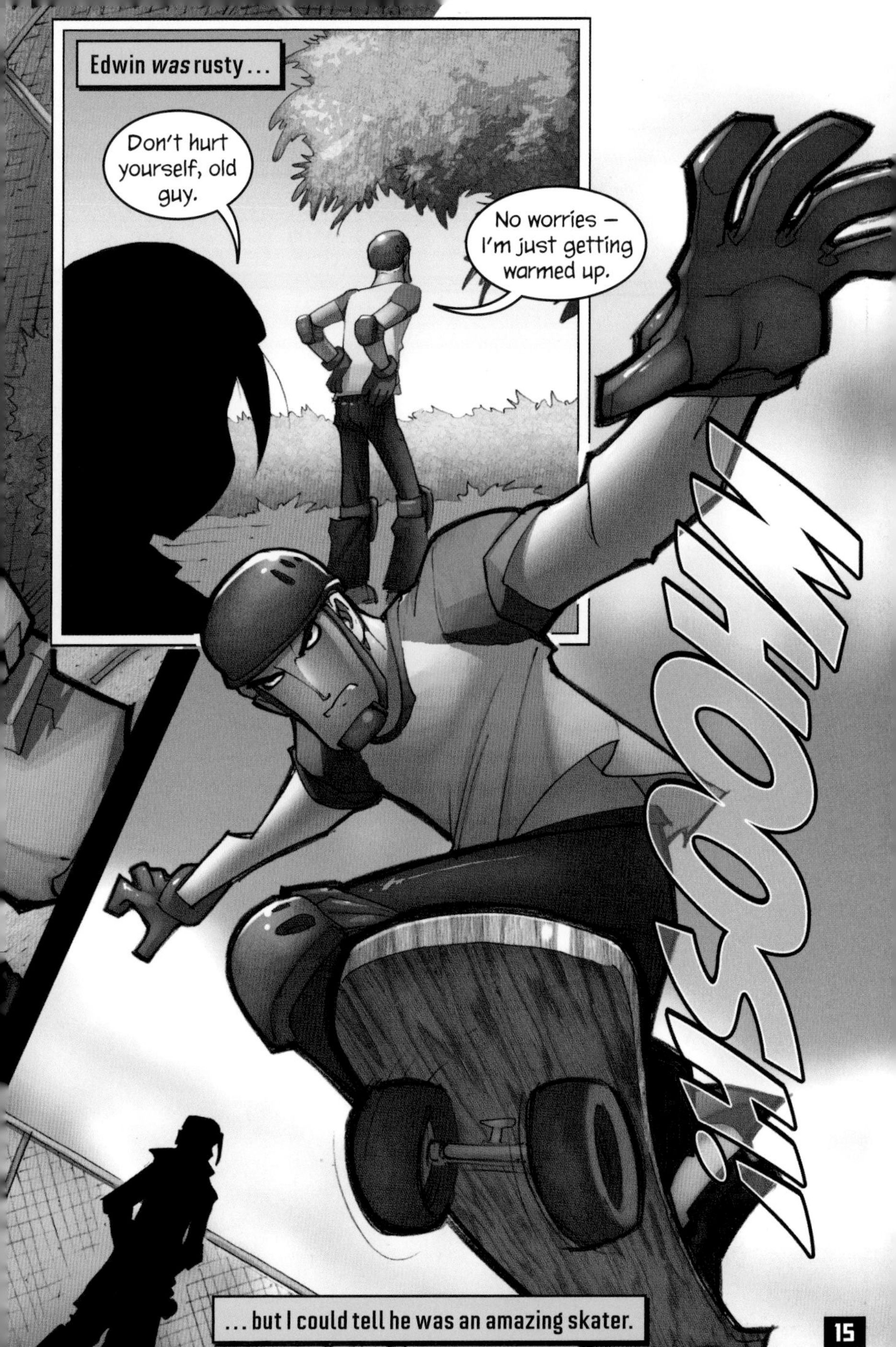
Edwin *was* rusty . . .
Don't hurt yourself, old guy.
No worries — I'm just getting warmed up.
WHOOSH!
. . . but I could tell he was an amazing skater.

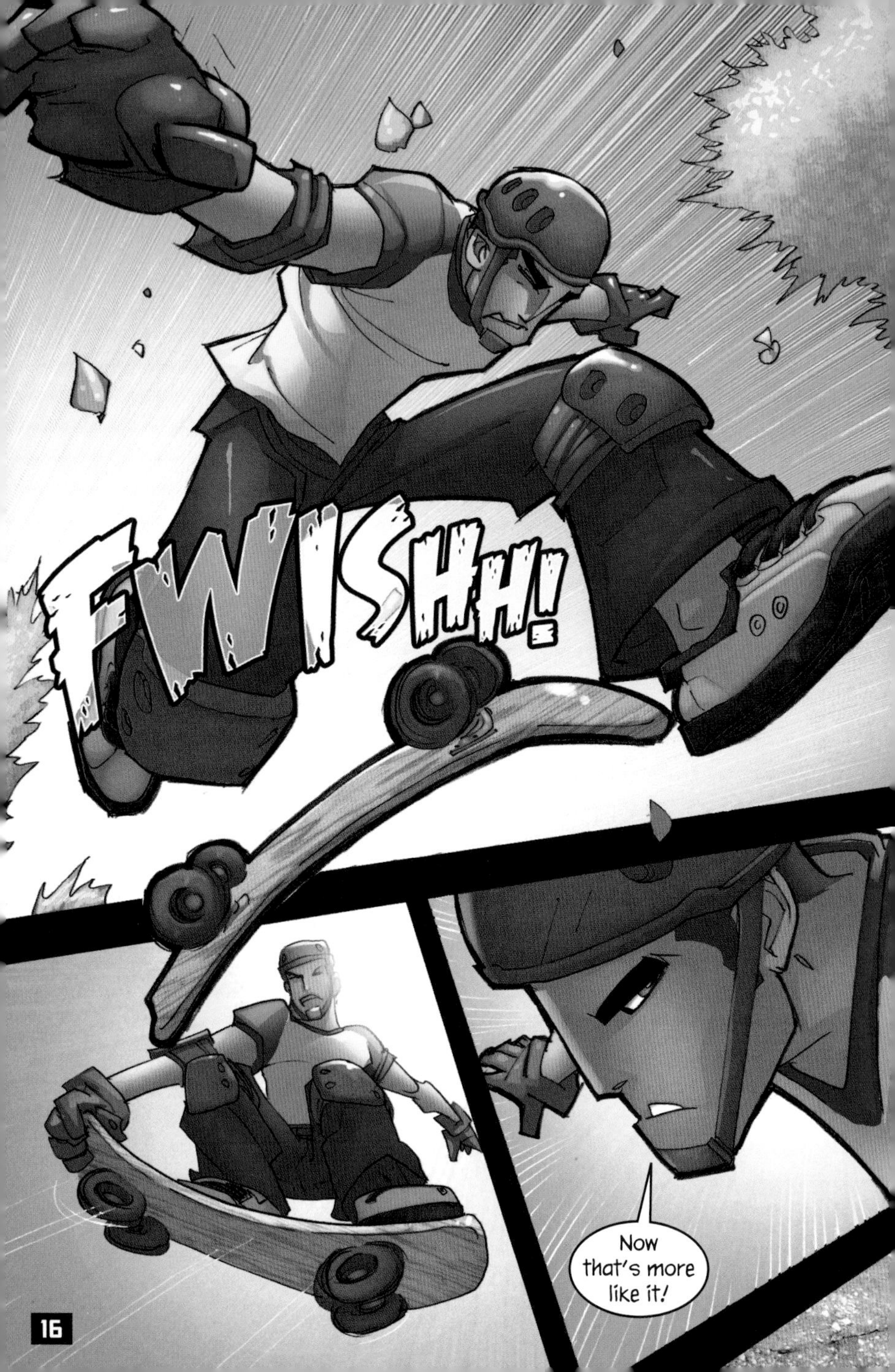
FWISHH!
Now that's more like it!

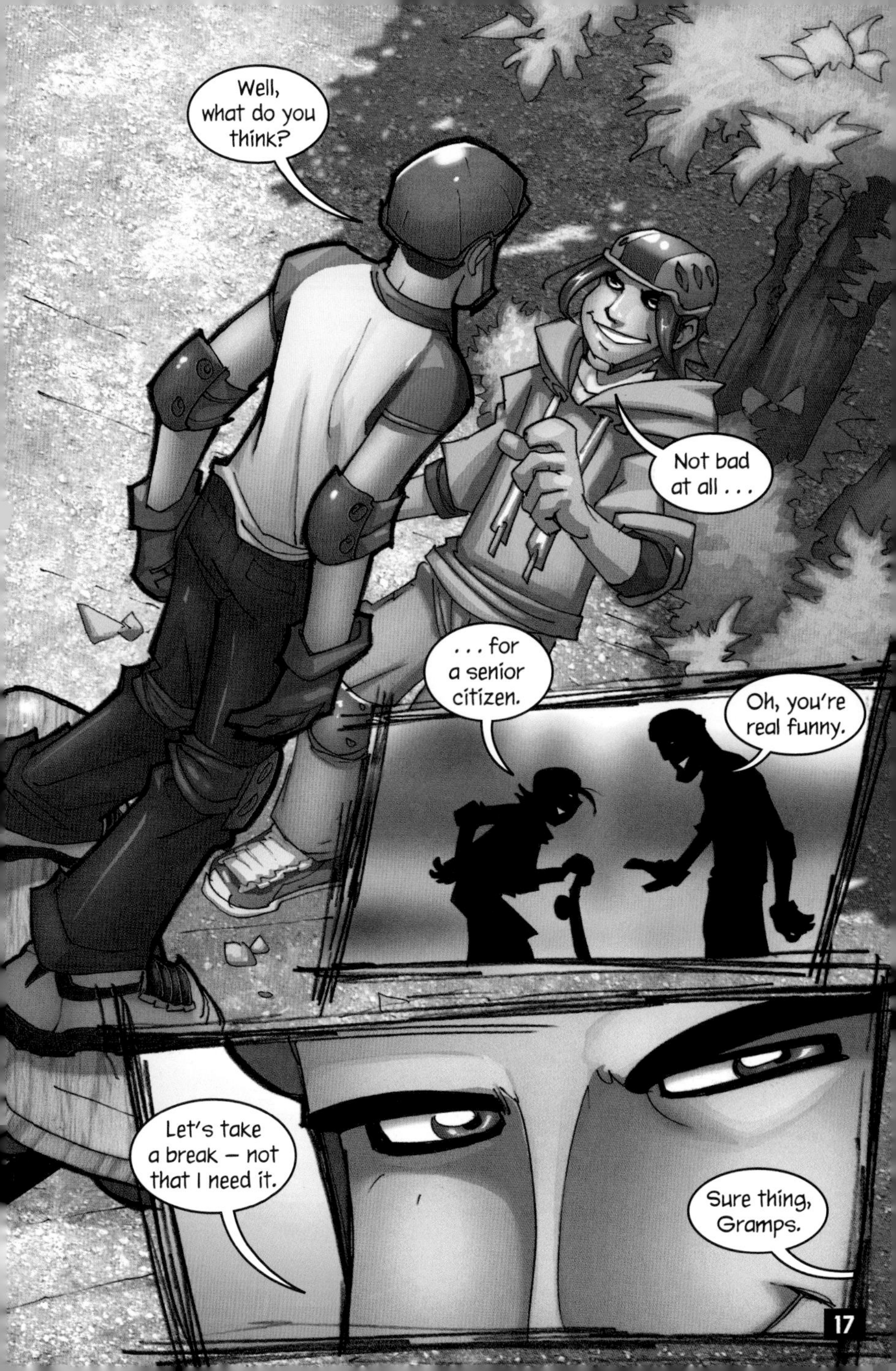
Well, what do you think?
Not bad at all . . .
. . . for a senior citizen.
Oh, you're real funny.
Let's take a break – not that I need it.
Sure thing, Gramps.

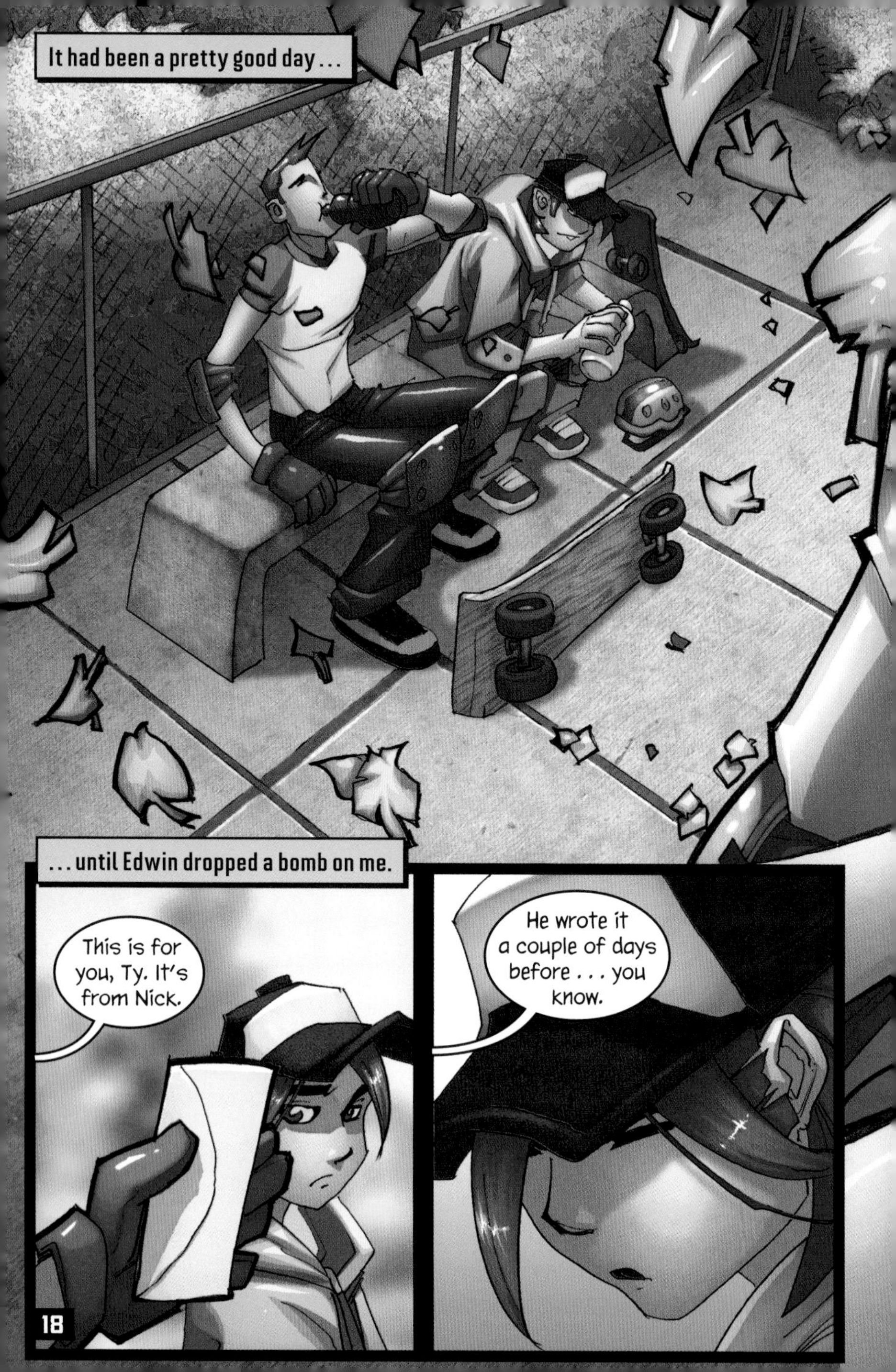
It had been a pretty good day . . .
. . . until Edwin dropped a bomb on me.
This is for you, Ty. It's from Nick.
He wrote it a couple of days before . . . you know.

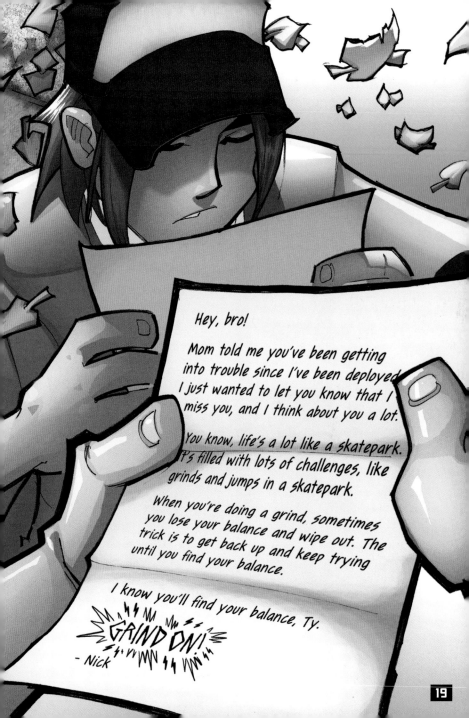

Hey, bro!

Mom told me you've been getting into trouble since I've been deployed. I just wanted to let you know that I miss you, and I think about you a lot.

You know, life's a lot like a skatepark. It's filled with lots of challenges, like grinds and jumps in a skatepark.

When you're doing a grind, sometimes you lose your balance and wipe out. The trick is to get back up and keep trying until you find your balance.

I know you'll find your balance, Ty.

GRIND ON!
- Nick

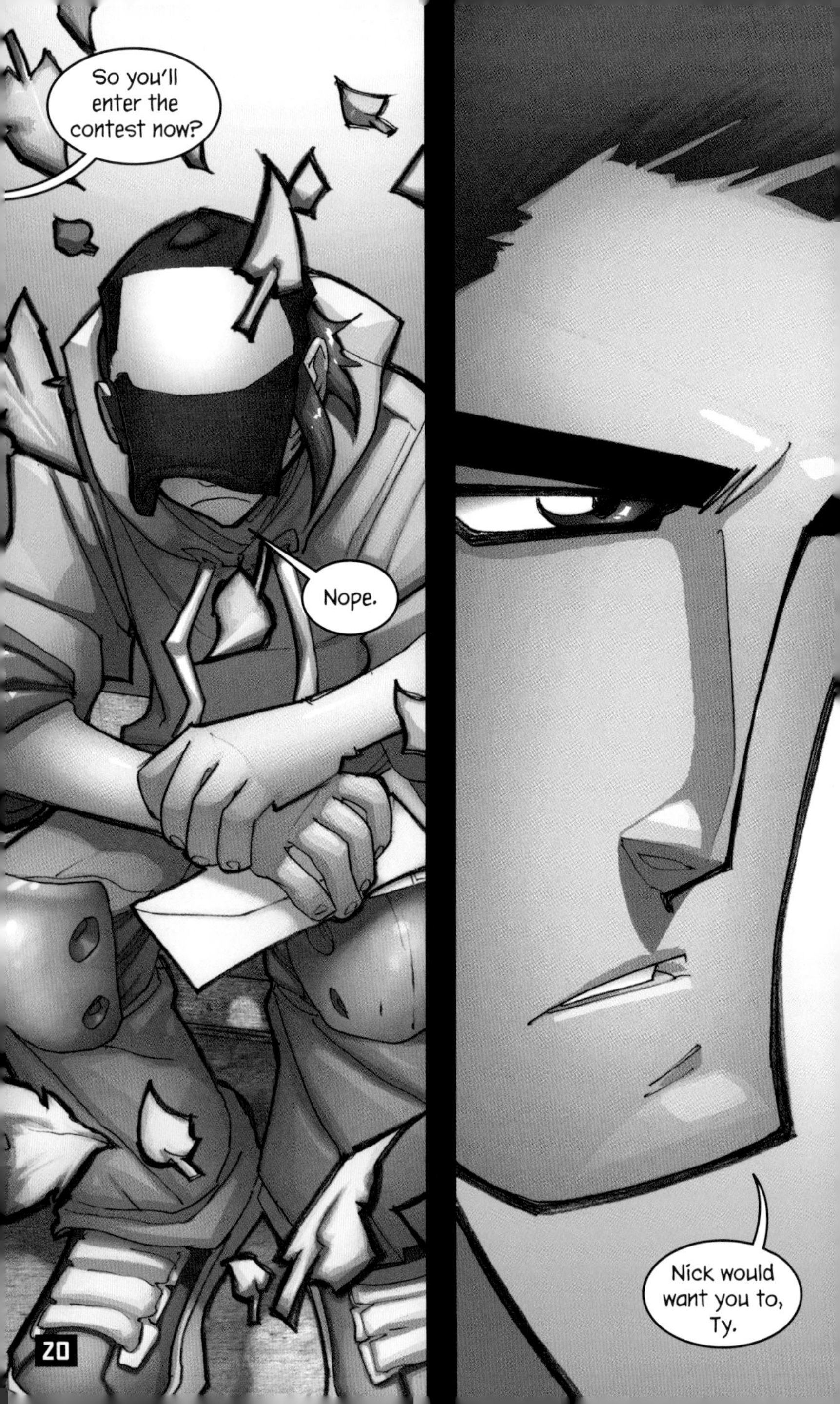
So you'll enter the contest now?
Nope.
Nick would want you to, Ty.

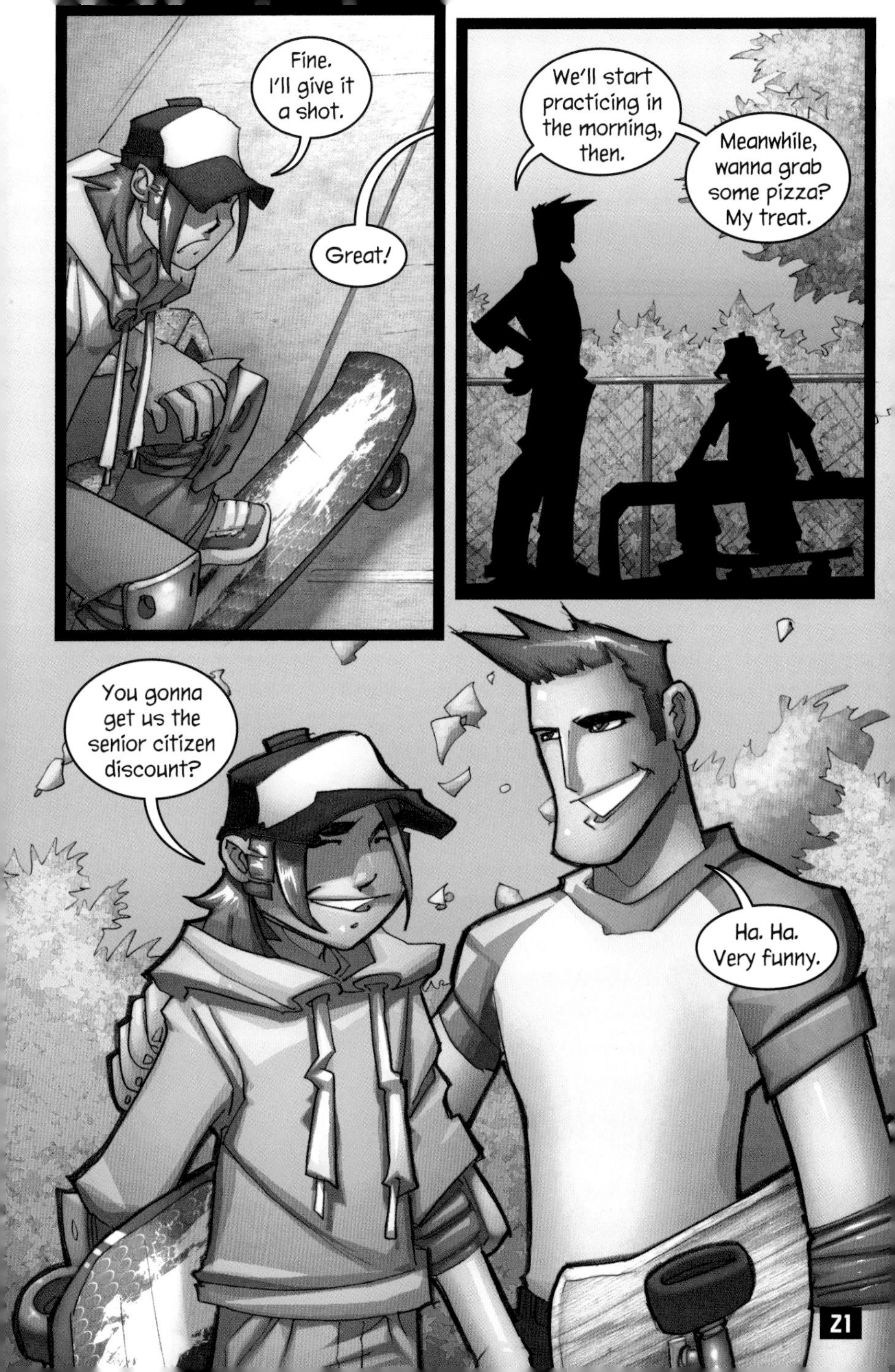
Fine. I'll give it a shot.
Great!
We'll start practicing in the morning, then.
Meanwhile, wanna grab some pizza? My treat.
You gonna get us the senior citizen discount?
Ha. Ha. Very funny.

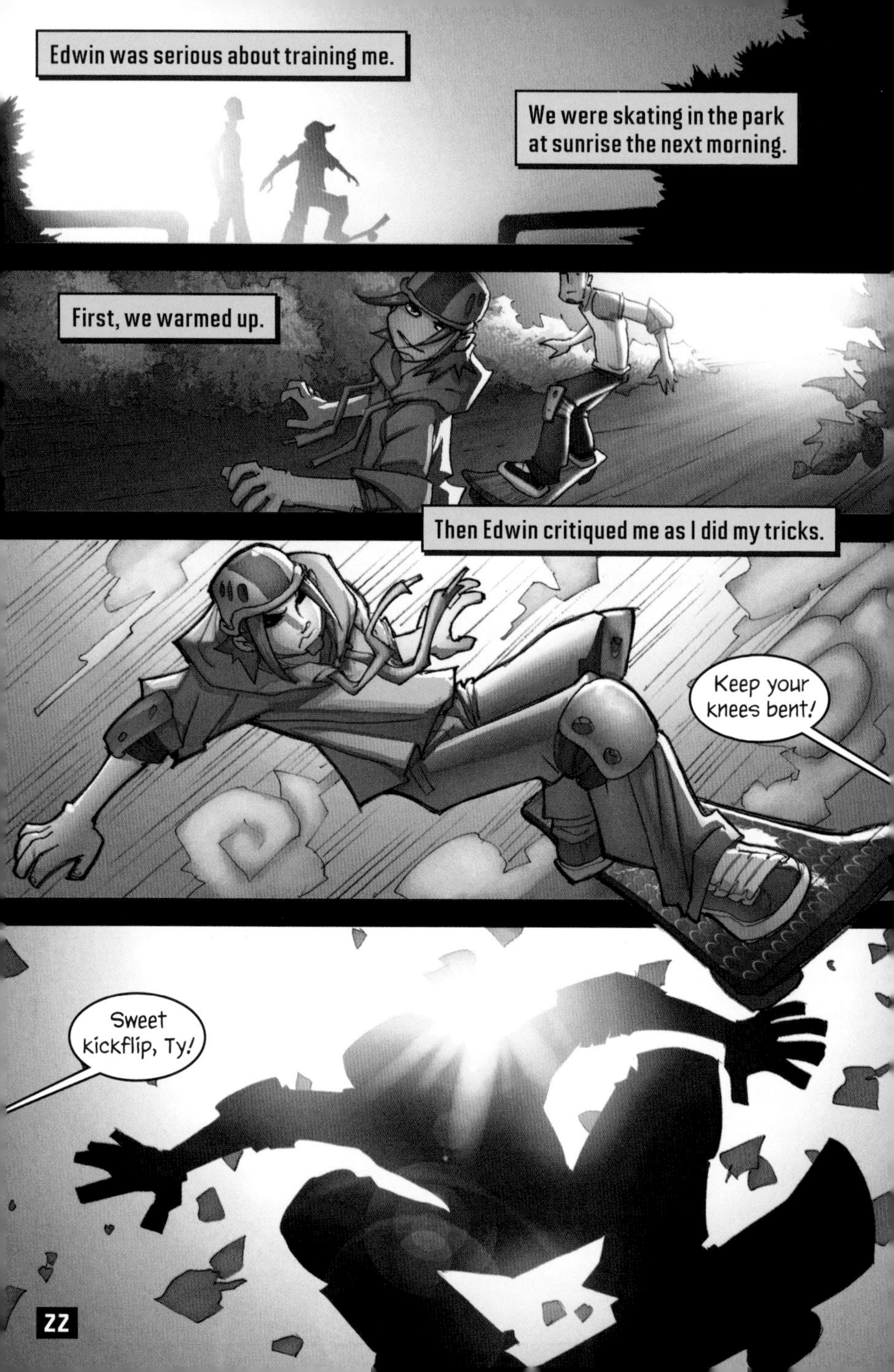
Edwin was serious about training me.
We were skating in the park at sunrise the next morning.
First, we warmed up.
Then Edwin critiqued me as I did my tricks.
Keep your knees bent!
Sweet kickflip, Ty!

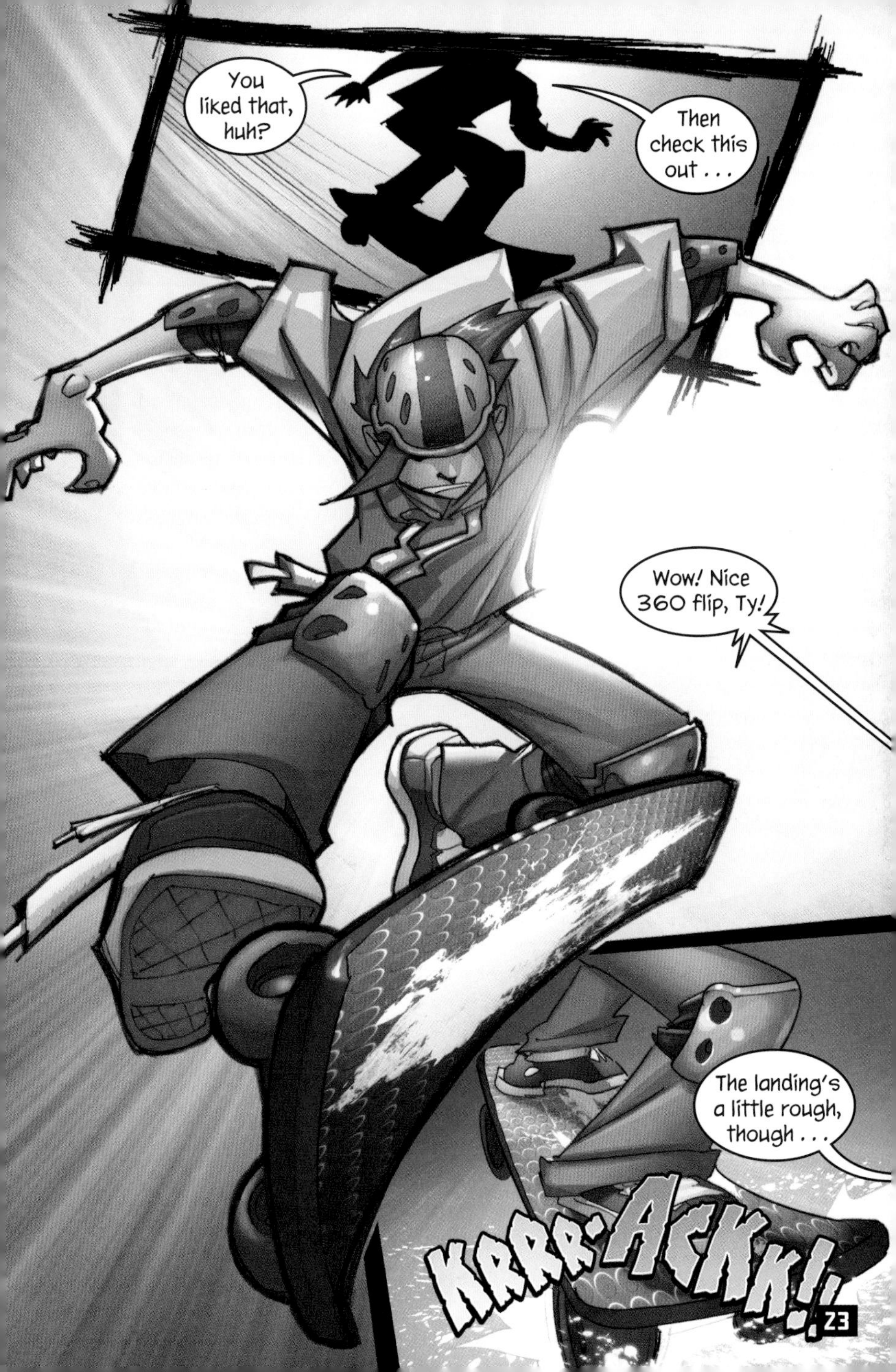
You liked that, huh?
Then check this out . . .
Wow! Nice 360 flip, Ty!
The landing's a little rough, though . . .
KRRR-ACKK!!

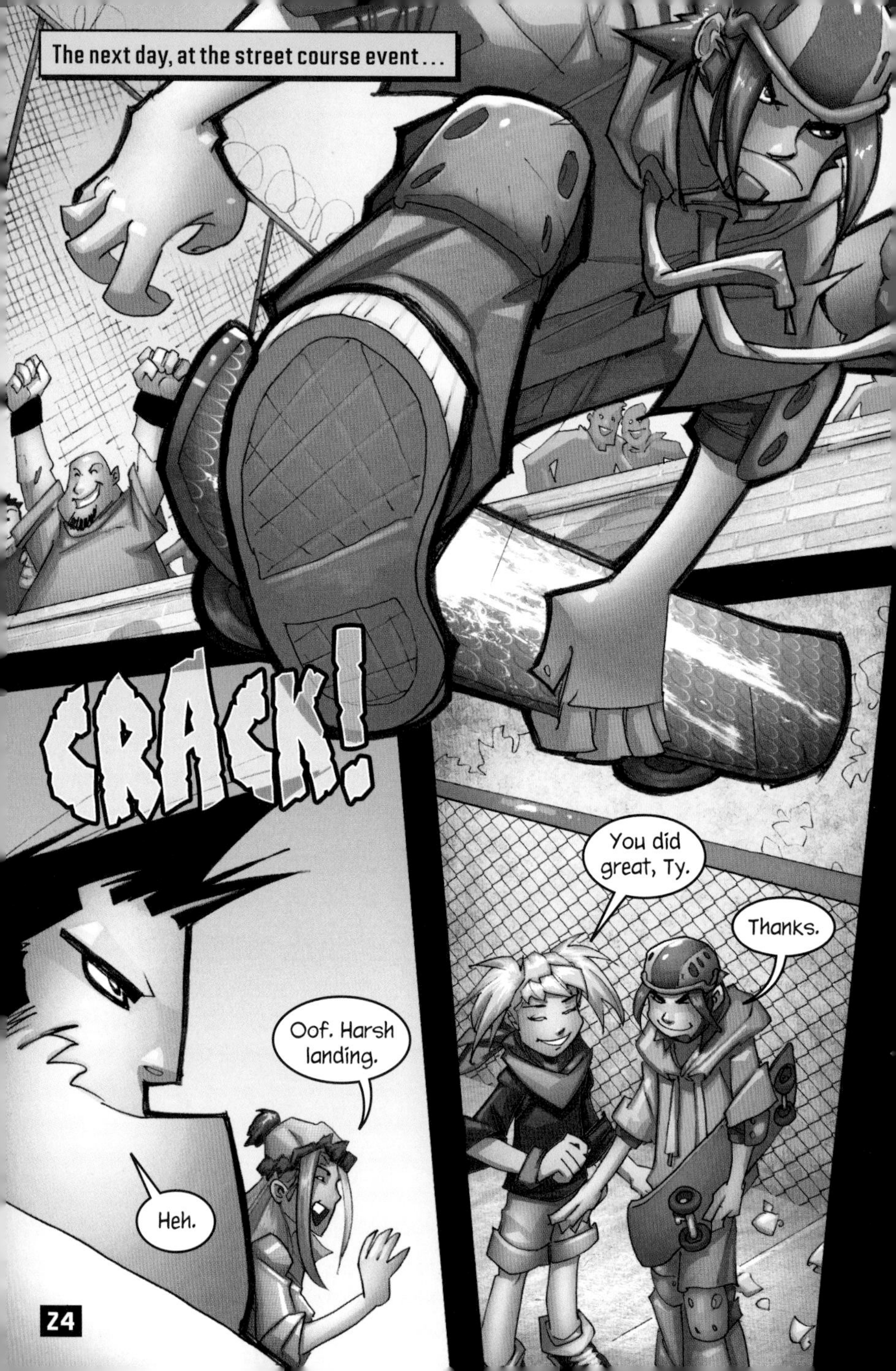
The next day, at the street course event . . .
CRACK!
Oof. Harsh landing.
Heh.
You did great, Ty.
Thanks.

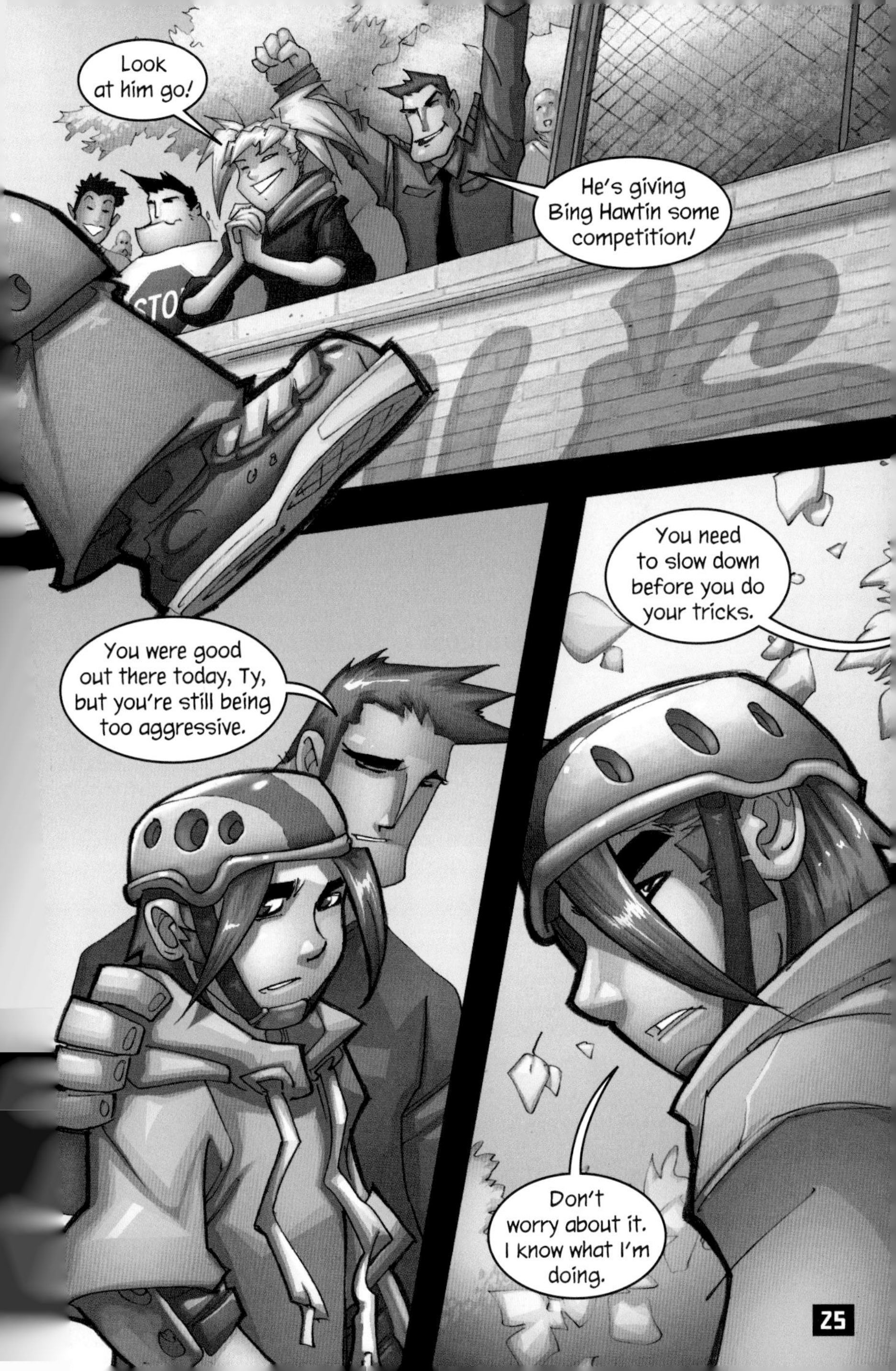

Look at him go!
He's giving Bing Hawtin some competition!
STO
You were good out there today, Ty, but you're still being too aggressive.
You need to slow down before you do your tricks.
Don't worry about it. I know what I'm doing.

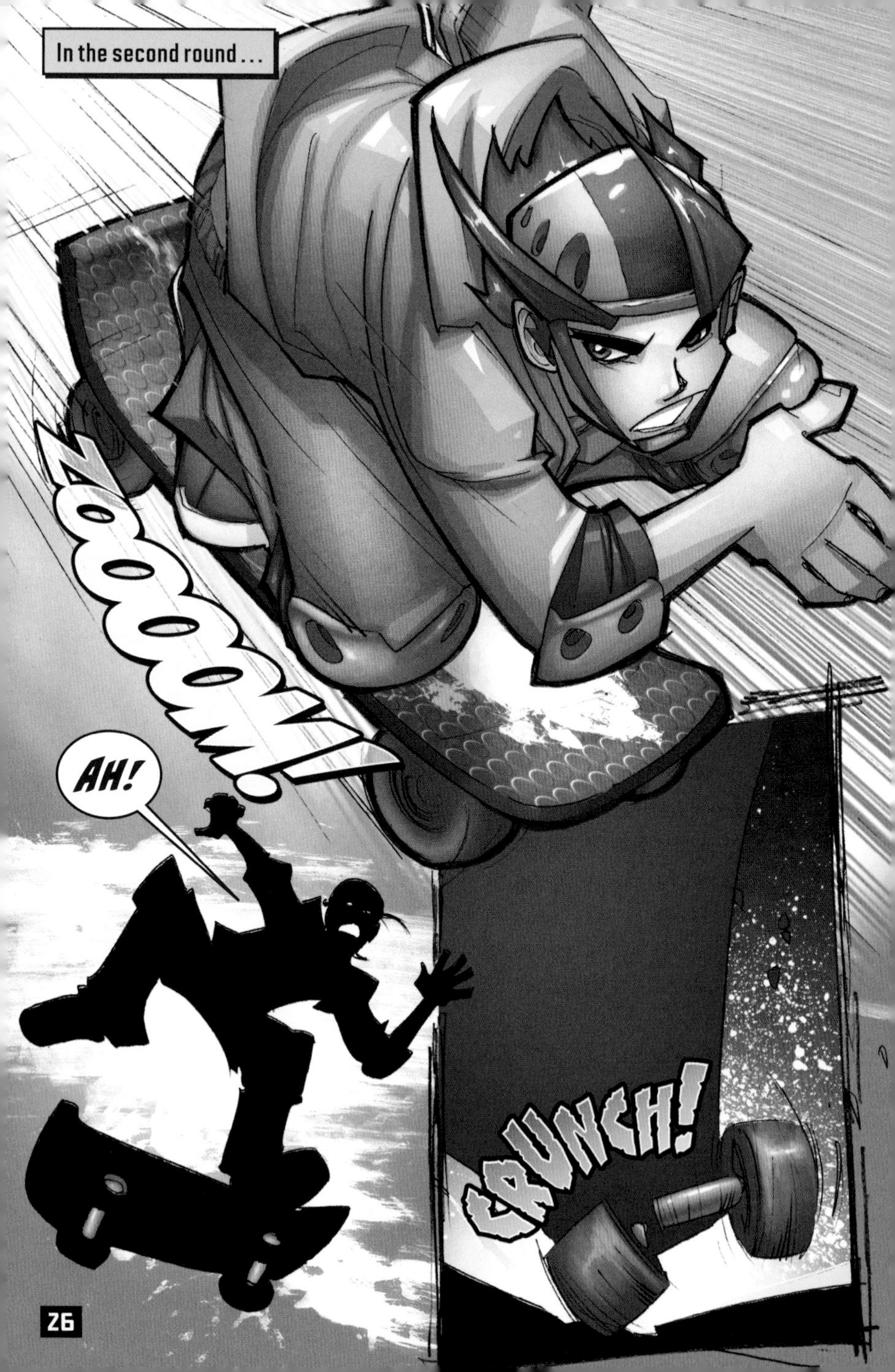
In the second round . . .
ZOOOOOOM!
AH!
CRUNCH!

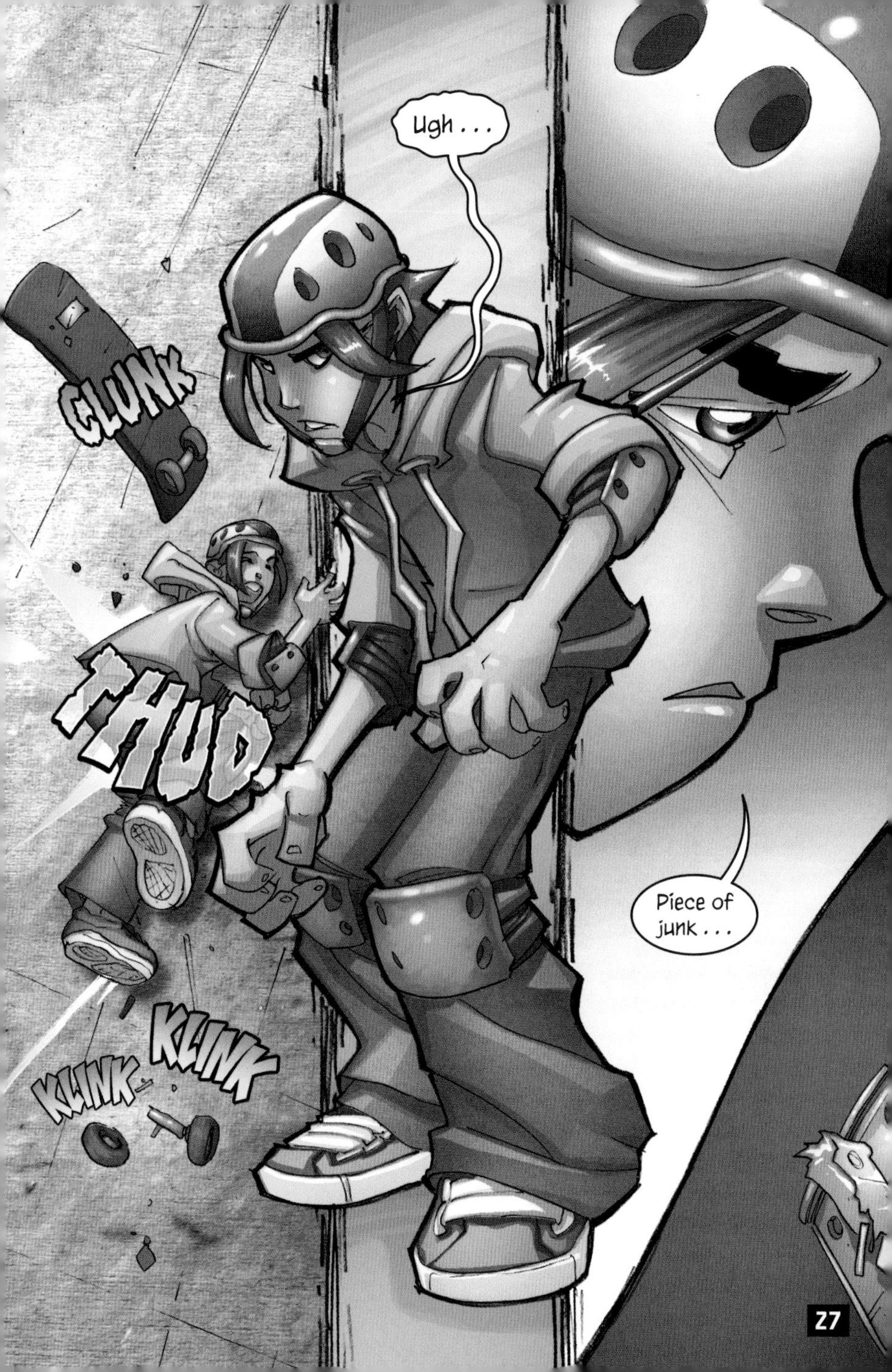
CLUNK
Ugh . . .
THUD
Piece of junk . . .
KLINK
KLINK

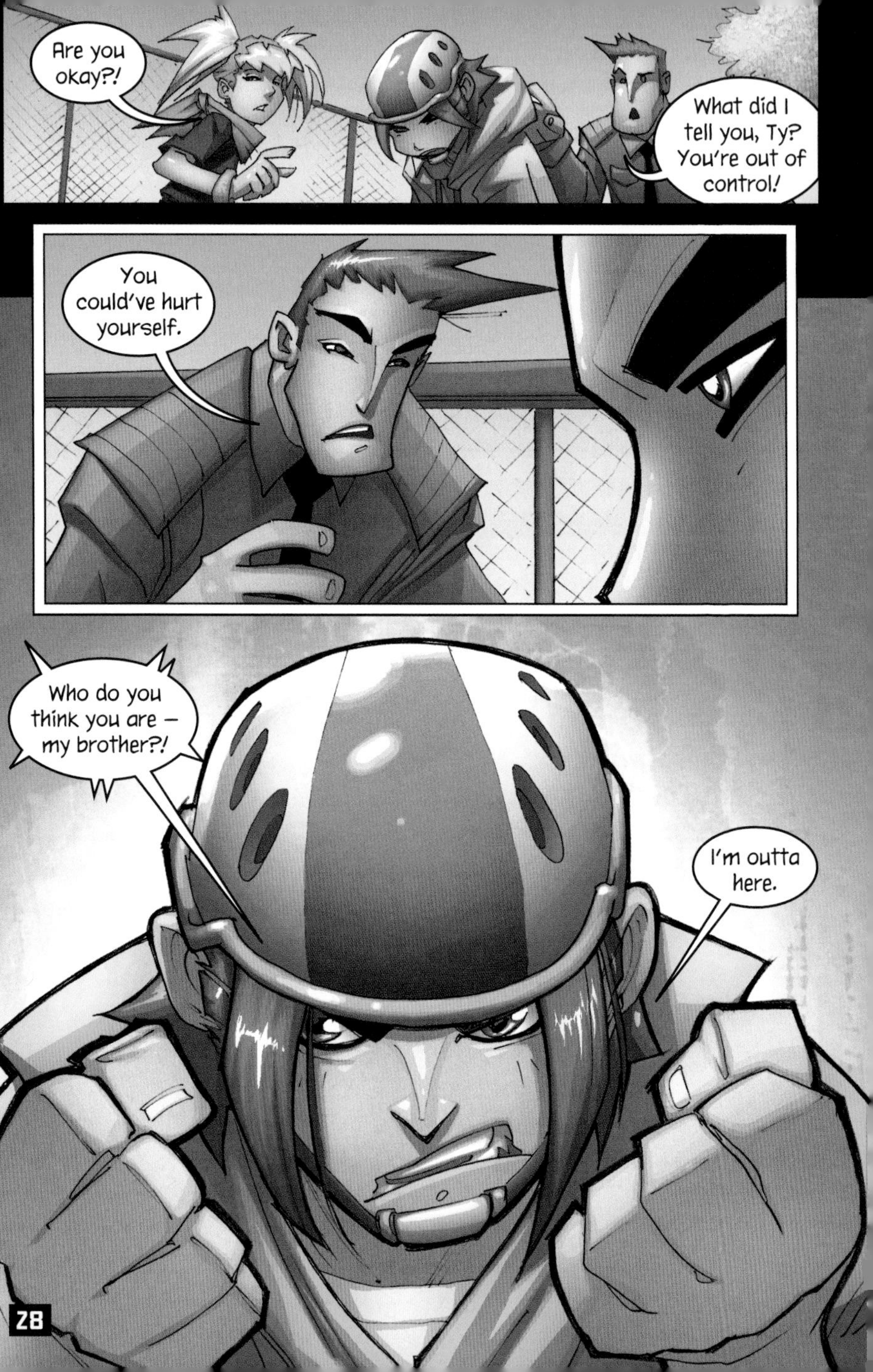
Are you okay?!
What did I tell you, Ty? You're out of control!
You could've hurt yourself.
Who do you think you are — my brother?!
I'm outta here.

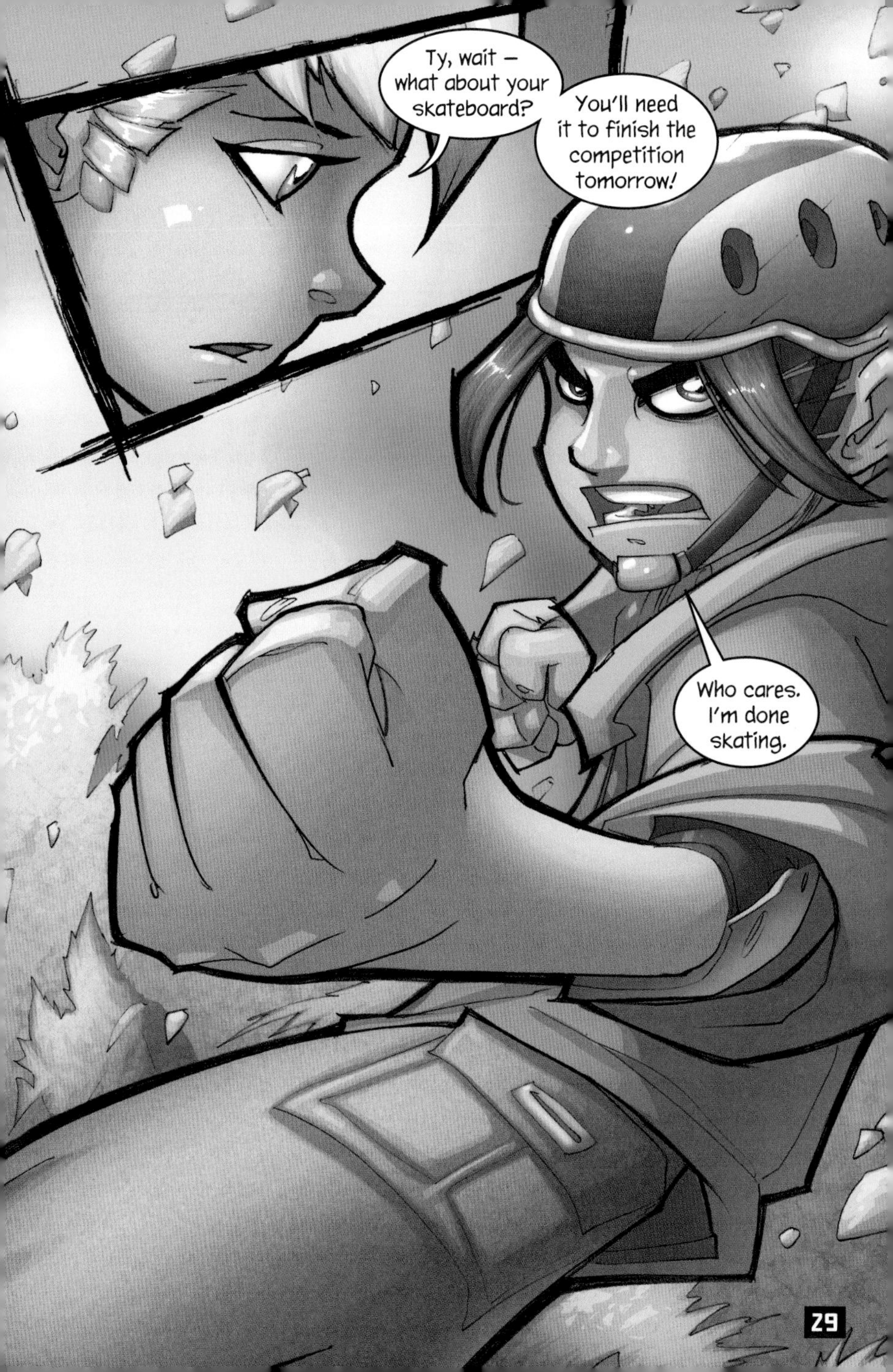
Ty, wait — what about your skateboard?
You'll need it to finish the competition tomorrow!
Who cares. I'm done skating.

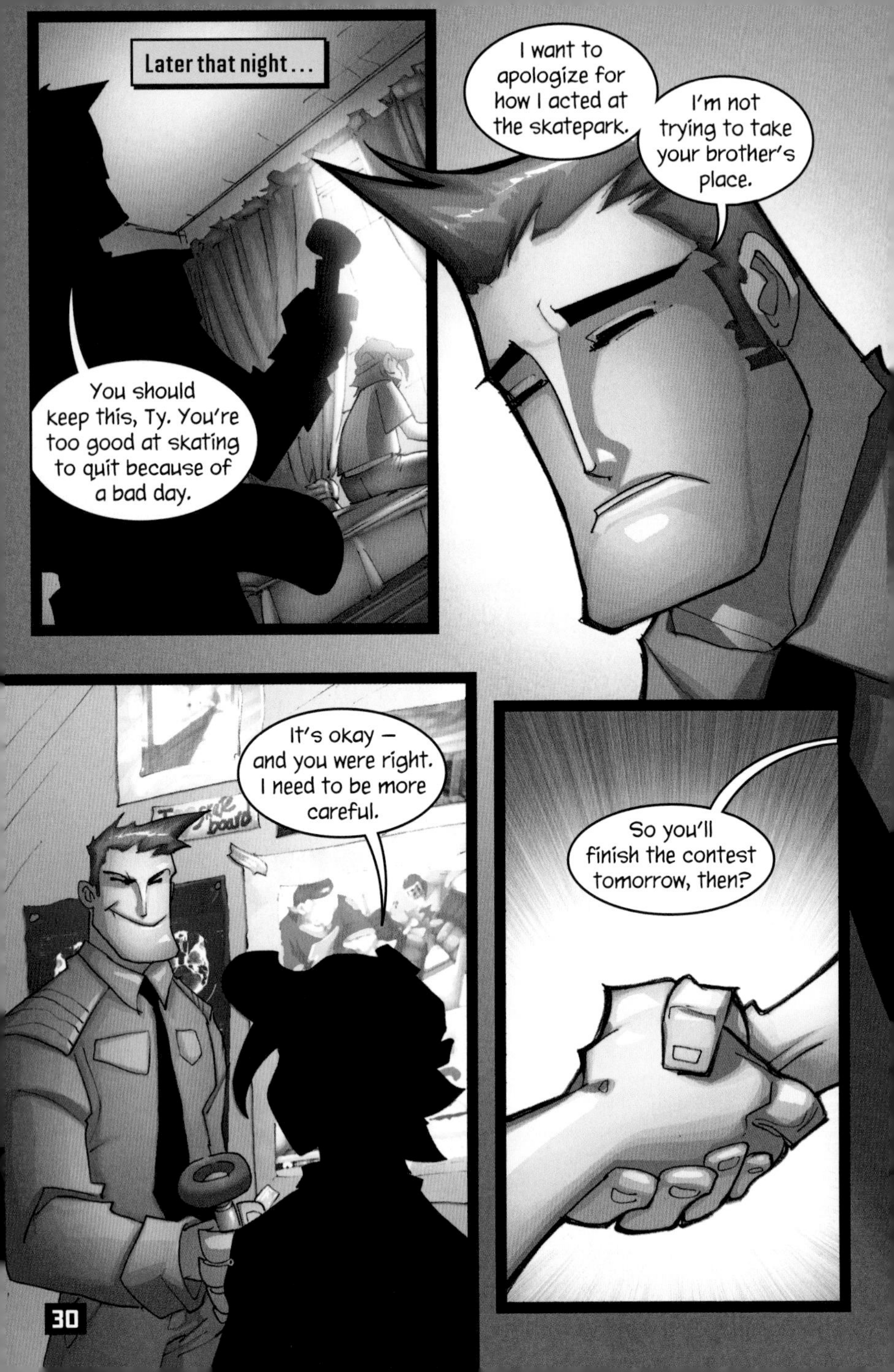
Later that night . . .
You should keep this, Ty. You're too good at skating to quit because of a bad day.
I want to apologize for how I acted at the skatepark.
I'm not trying to take your brother's place.
It's okay — and you were right. I need to be more careful.
So you'll finish the contest tomorrow, then?

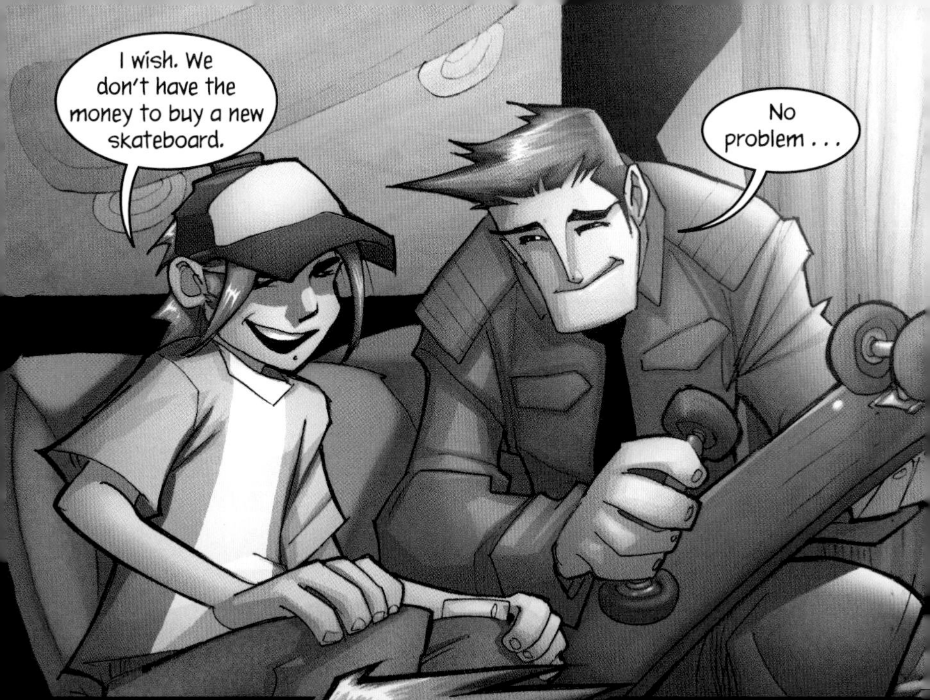
I wish. We don't have the money to buy a new skateboard.
No problem . . .

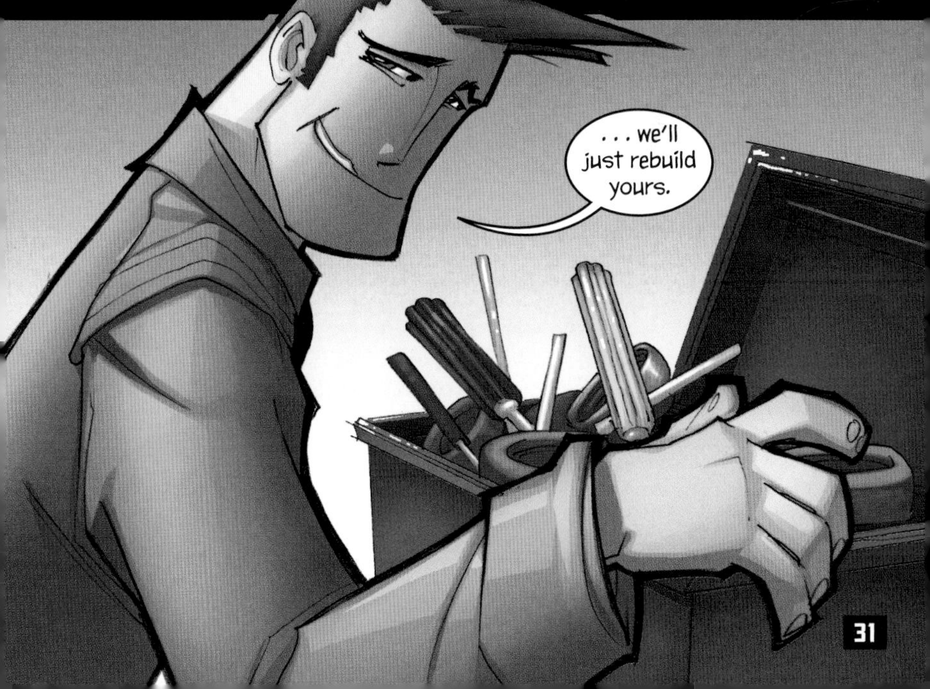
. . . we'll just rebuild yours.

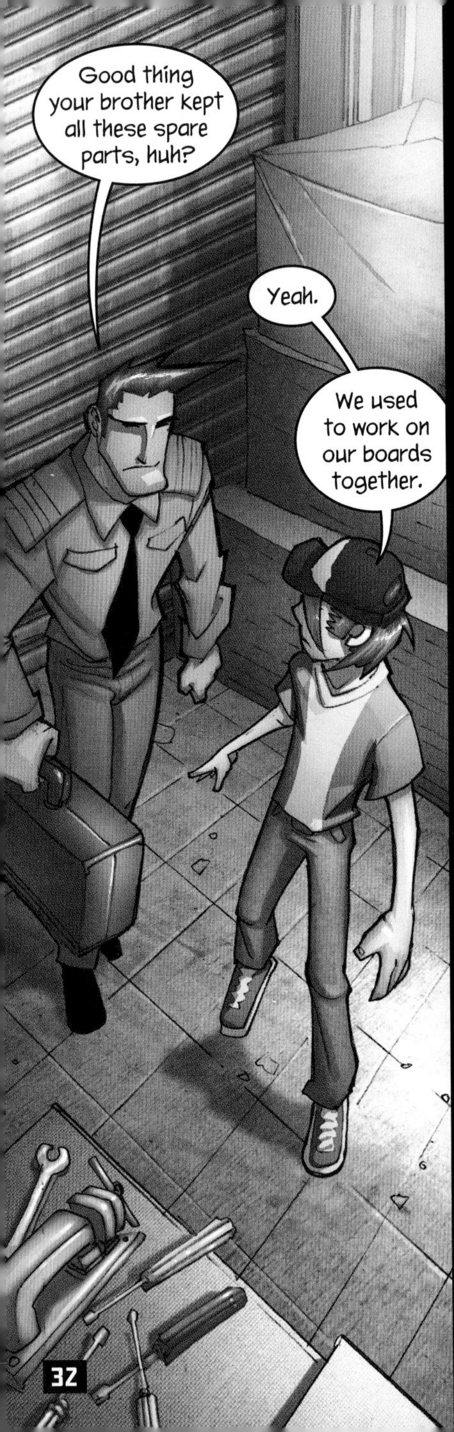
Good thing your brother kept all these spare parts, huh?
Yeah.
We used to work on our boards together.

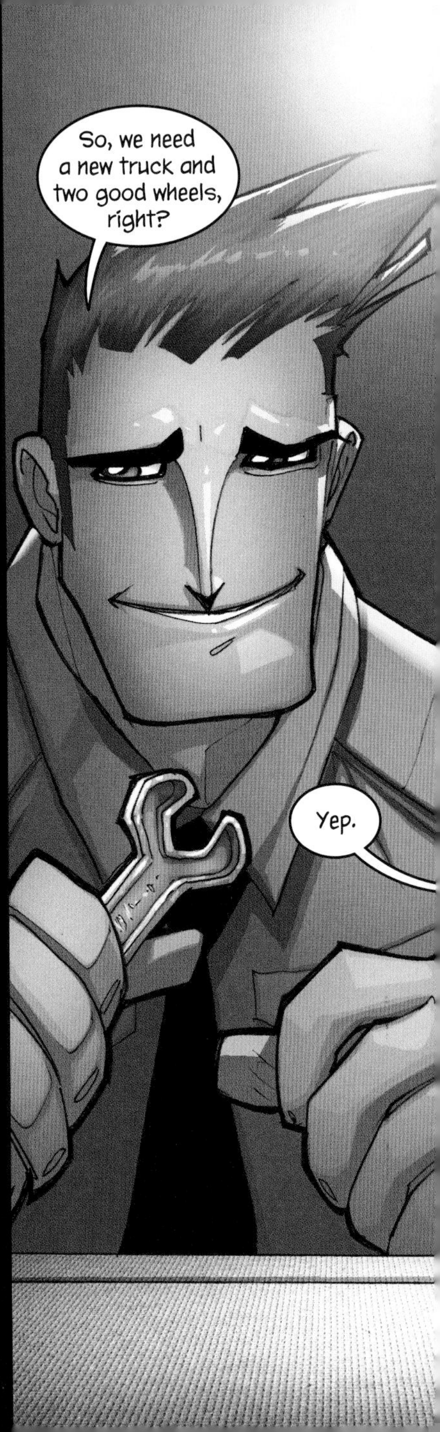
So, we need a new truck and two good wheels, right?
Yep.

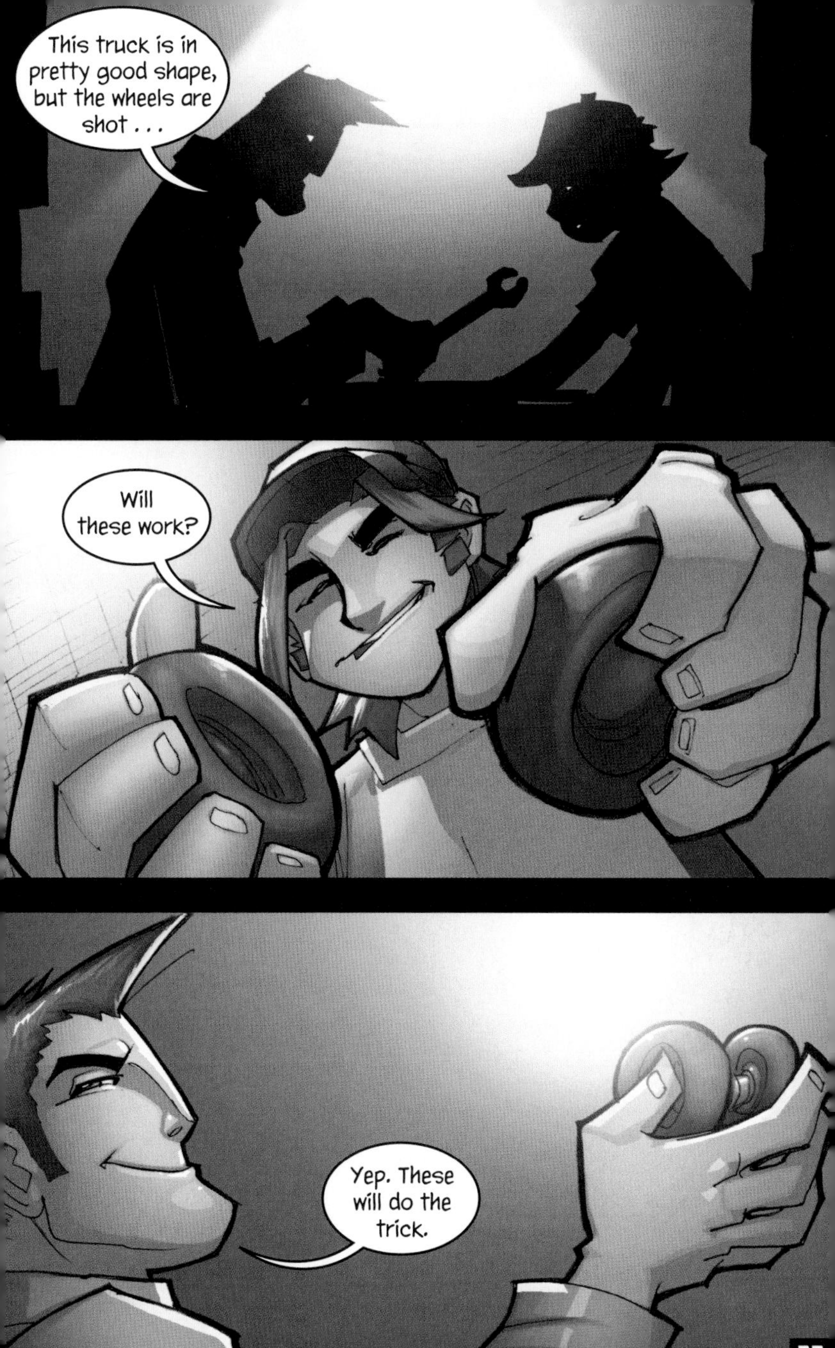
This truck is in pretty good shape, but the wheels are shot . . .
Will these work?
Yep. These will do the trick.

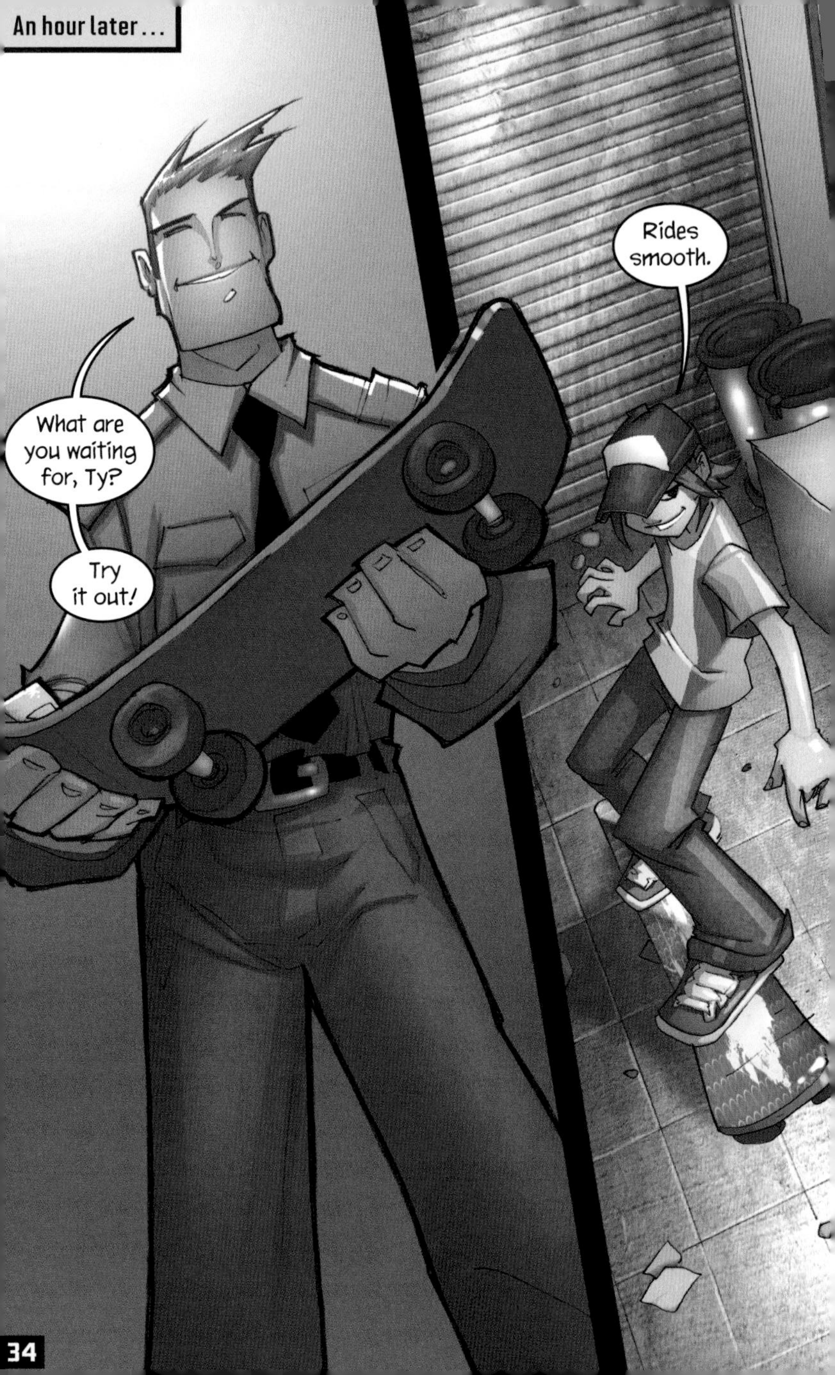
An hour later . . .
What are you waiting for, Ty?
Try it out!
Rides smooth.

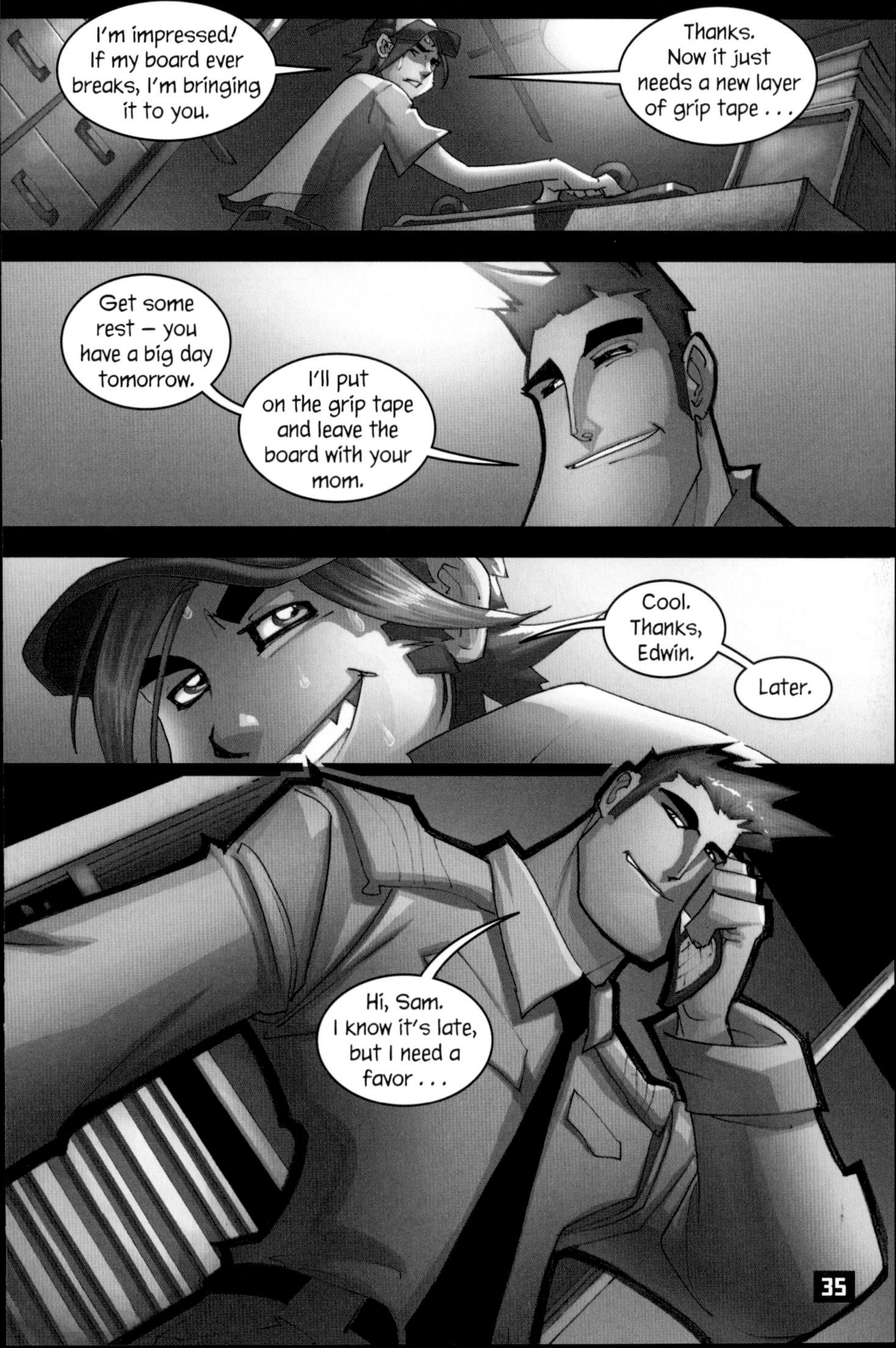
I'm impressed! If my board ever breaks, I'm bringing it to you.
Thanks. Now it just needs a new layer of grip tape . . .
Get some rest – you have a big day tomorrow.
I'll put on the grip tape and leave the board with your mom.
Cool. Thanks, Edwin.
Later.
Hi, Sam. I know it's late, but I need a favor . . .

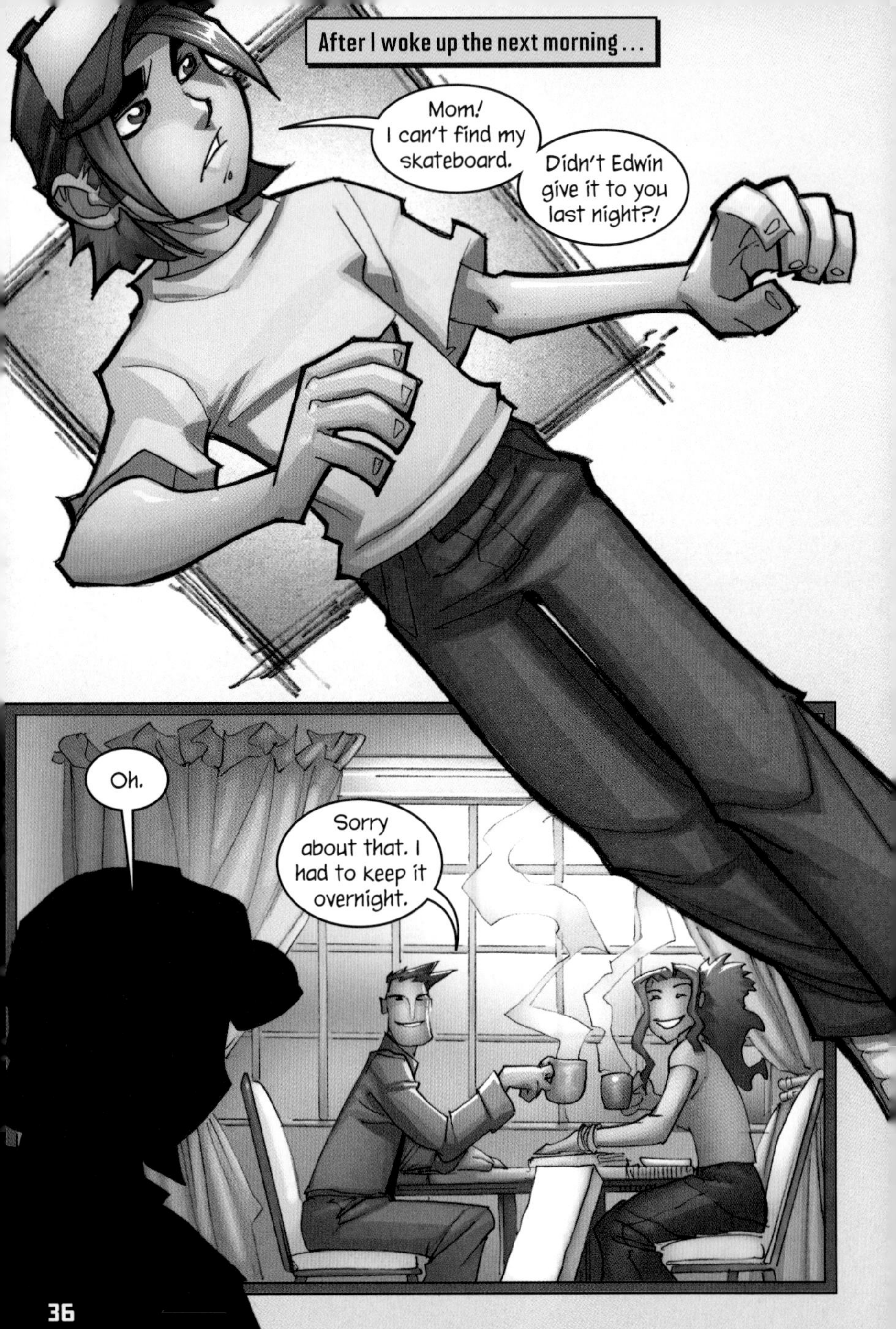
After I woke up the next morning . . .
Mom! I can't find my skateboard.
Didn't Edwin give it to you last night?!
Oh.
Sorry about that. I had to keep it overnight.

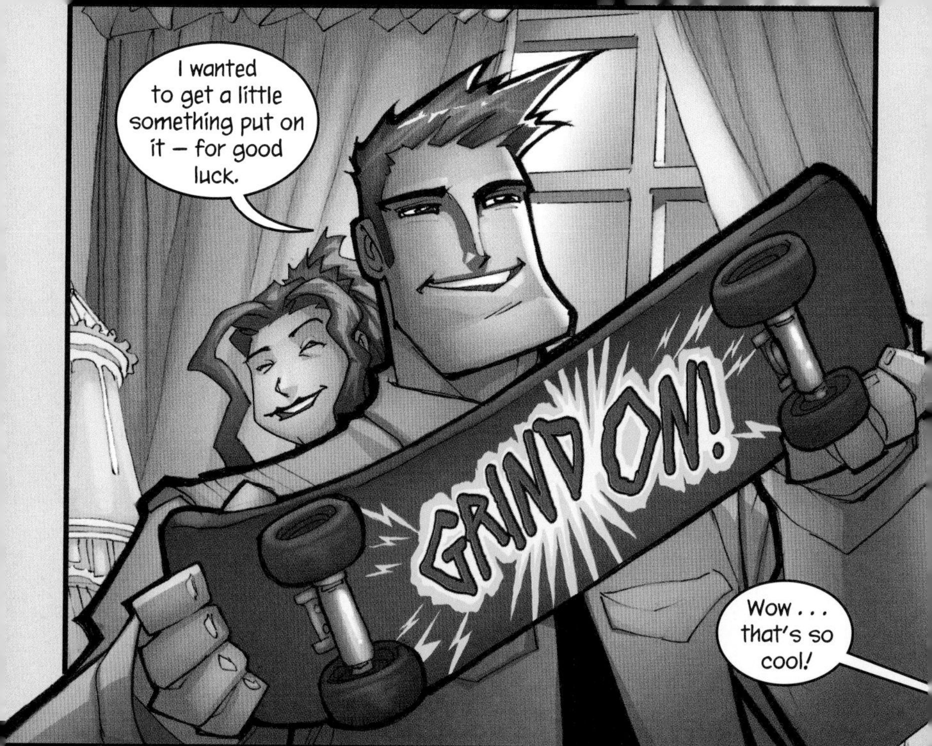
I wanted to get a little something put on it — for good luck.
GRIND ON!
Wow . . . that's so cool!

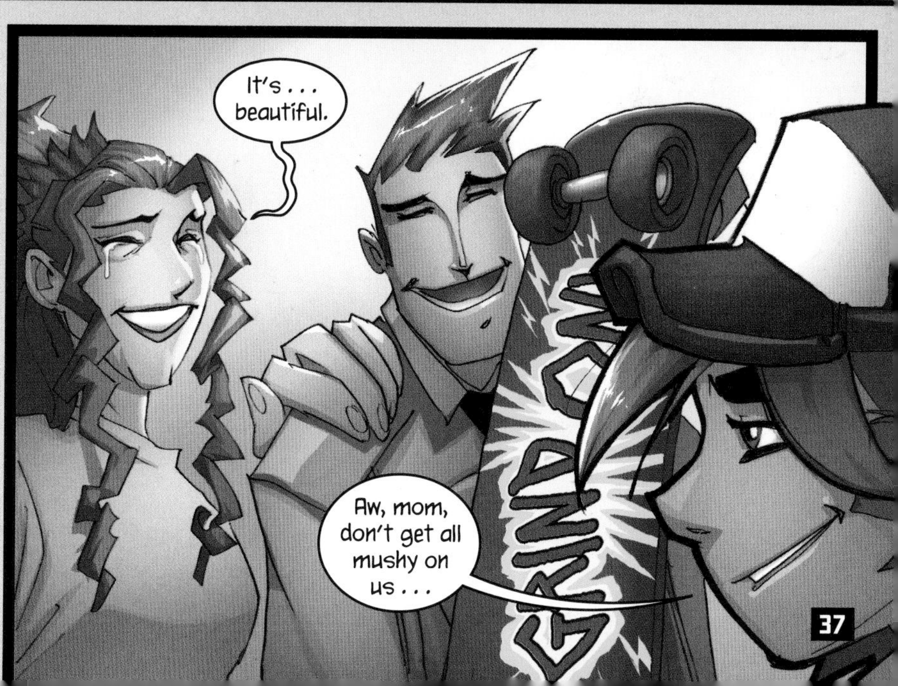
It's . . . beautiful.
Aw, mom, don't get all mushy on us . . .

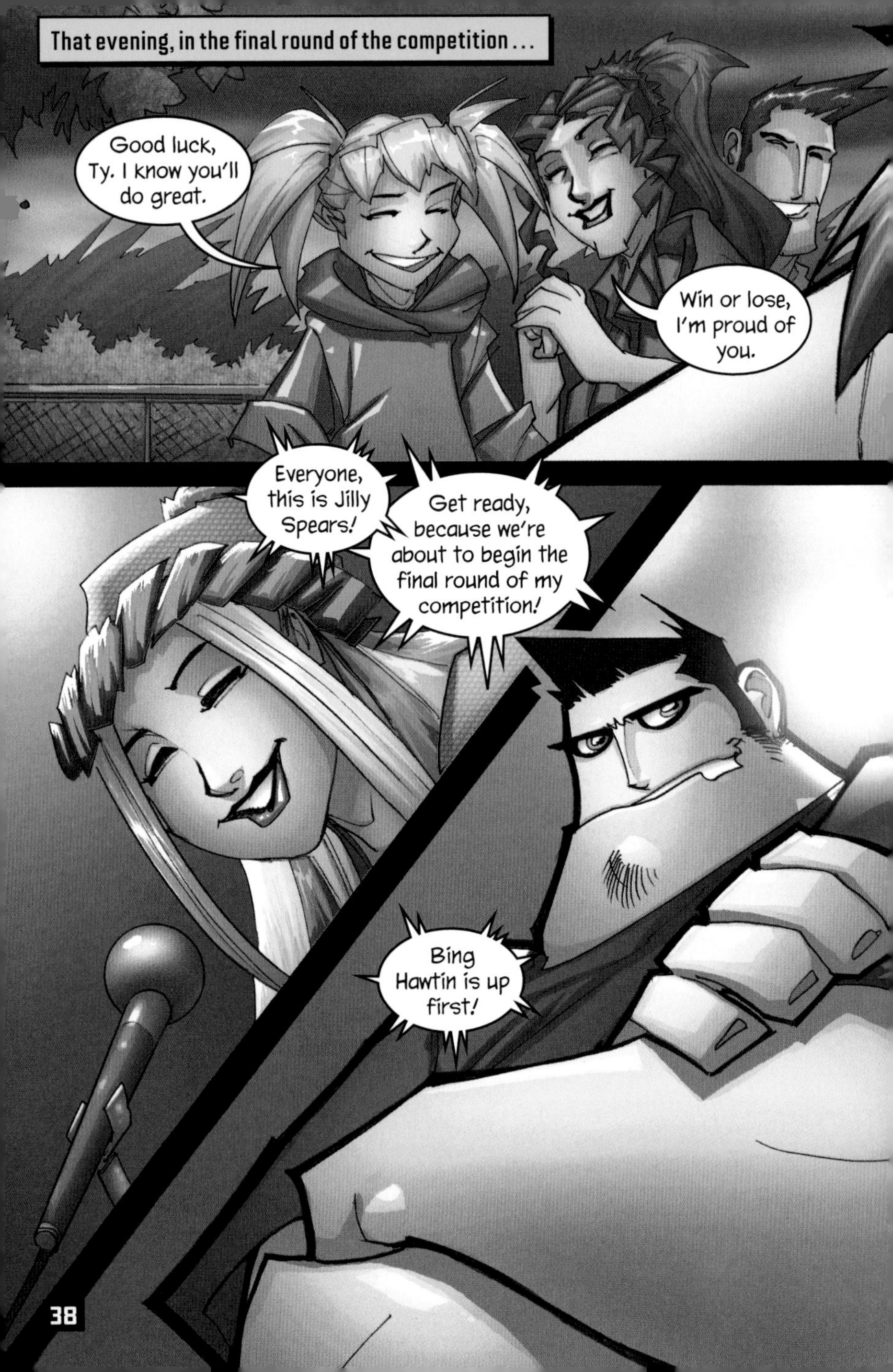
That evening, in the final round of the competition . . .
Good luck, Ty. I know you'll do great.
Win or lose, I'm proud of you.
Everyone, this is Jilly Spears!
Get ready, because we're about to begin the final round of my competition!
Bing Hawtin is up first!

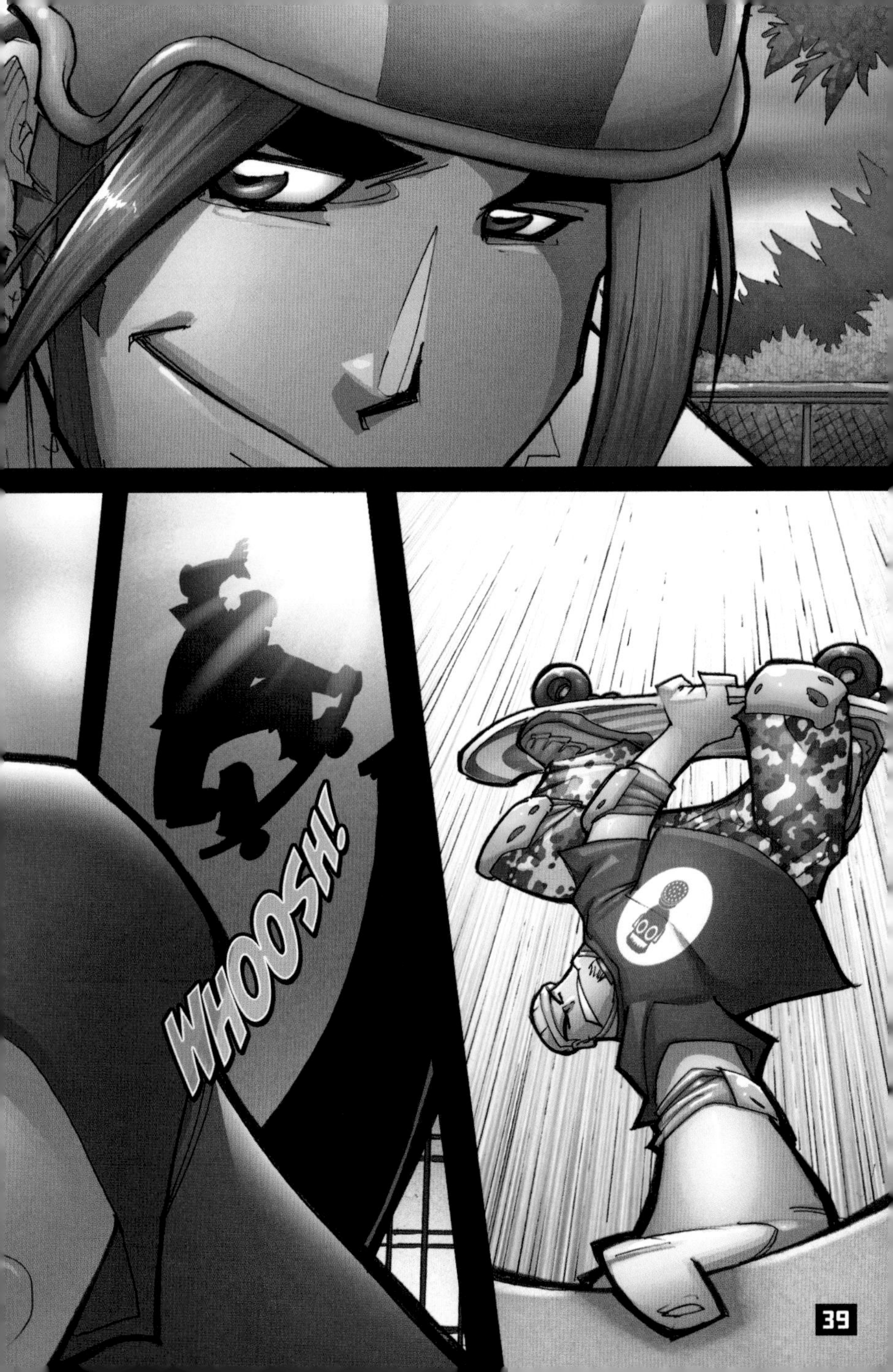
WHOOSH!

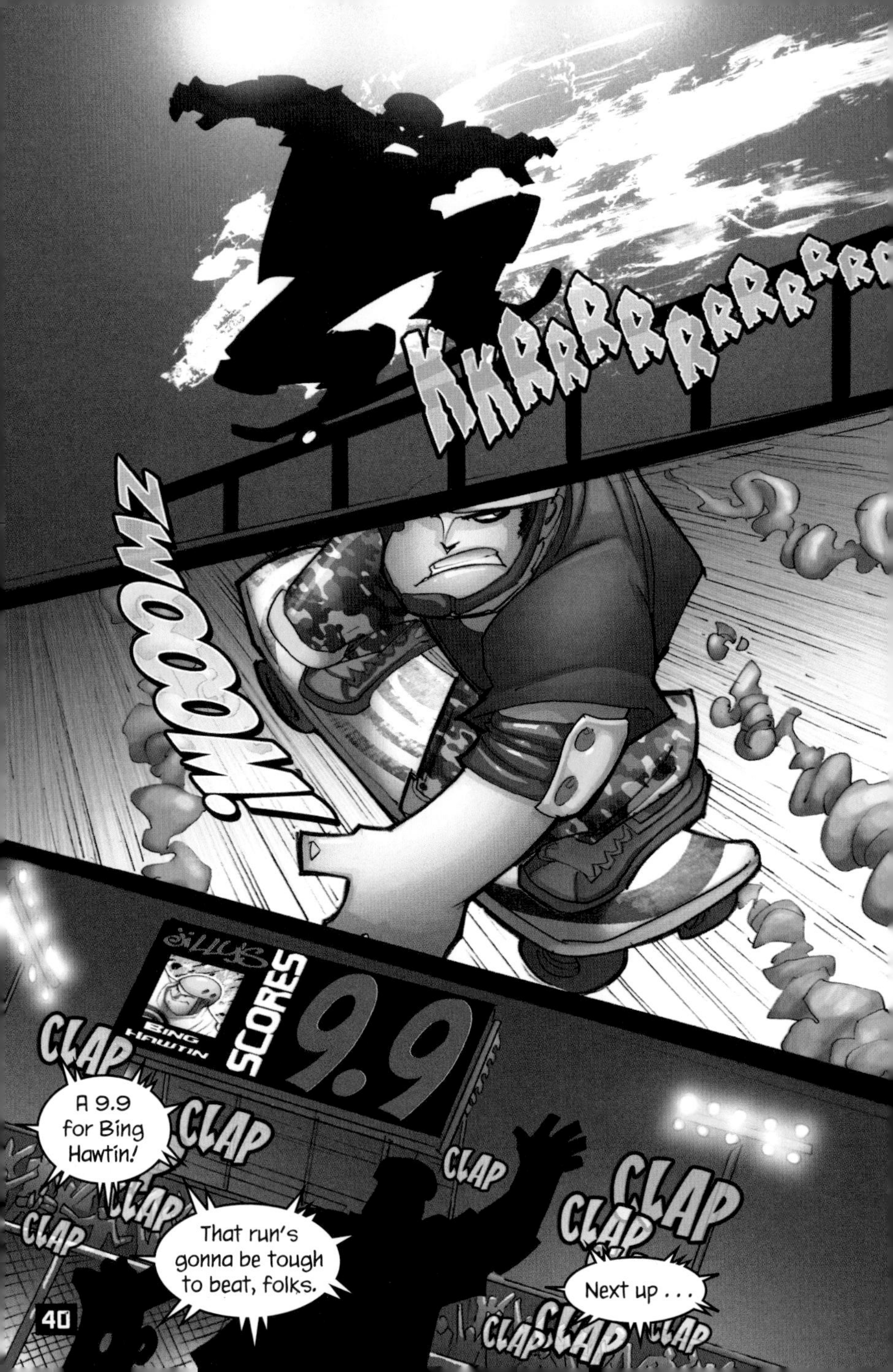
KKRRRRRRRRRR
ZWOOOM!
BING HAWTIN
SCORES 9.9
CLAP
A 9.9 for Bing Hawtin!
CLAP
CLAP
CLAP
CLAP
CLAP
CLAP
CLAP
That run's gonna be tough to beat, folks.
Next up . . .
CLAP CLAP CLAP CLAP

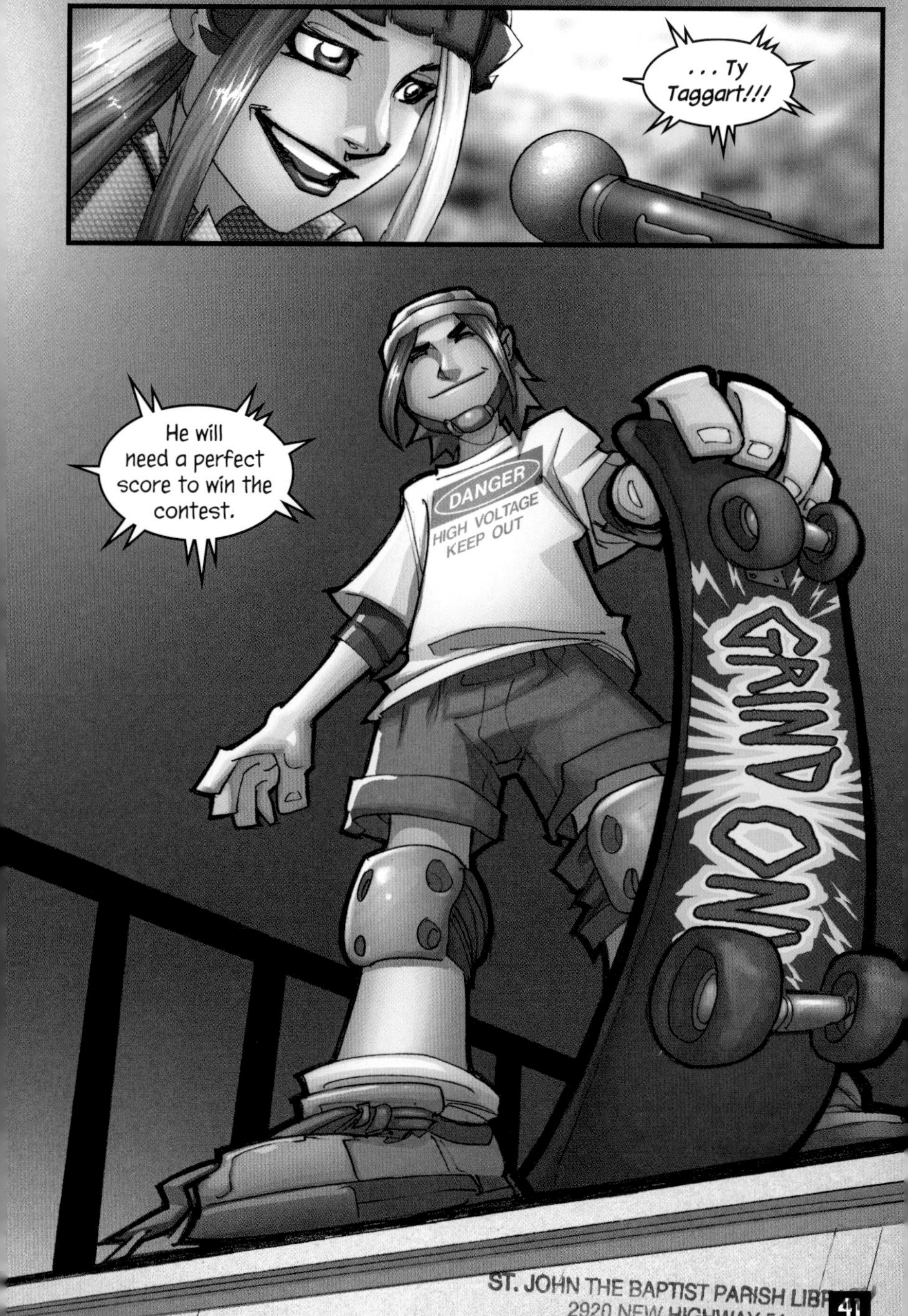
. . . Ty Taggart!!!
He will need a perfect score to win the contest.
DANGER
HIGH VOLTAGE
KEEP OUT
GRIND ON

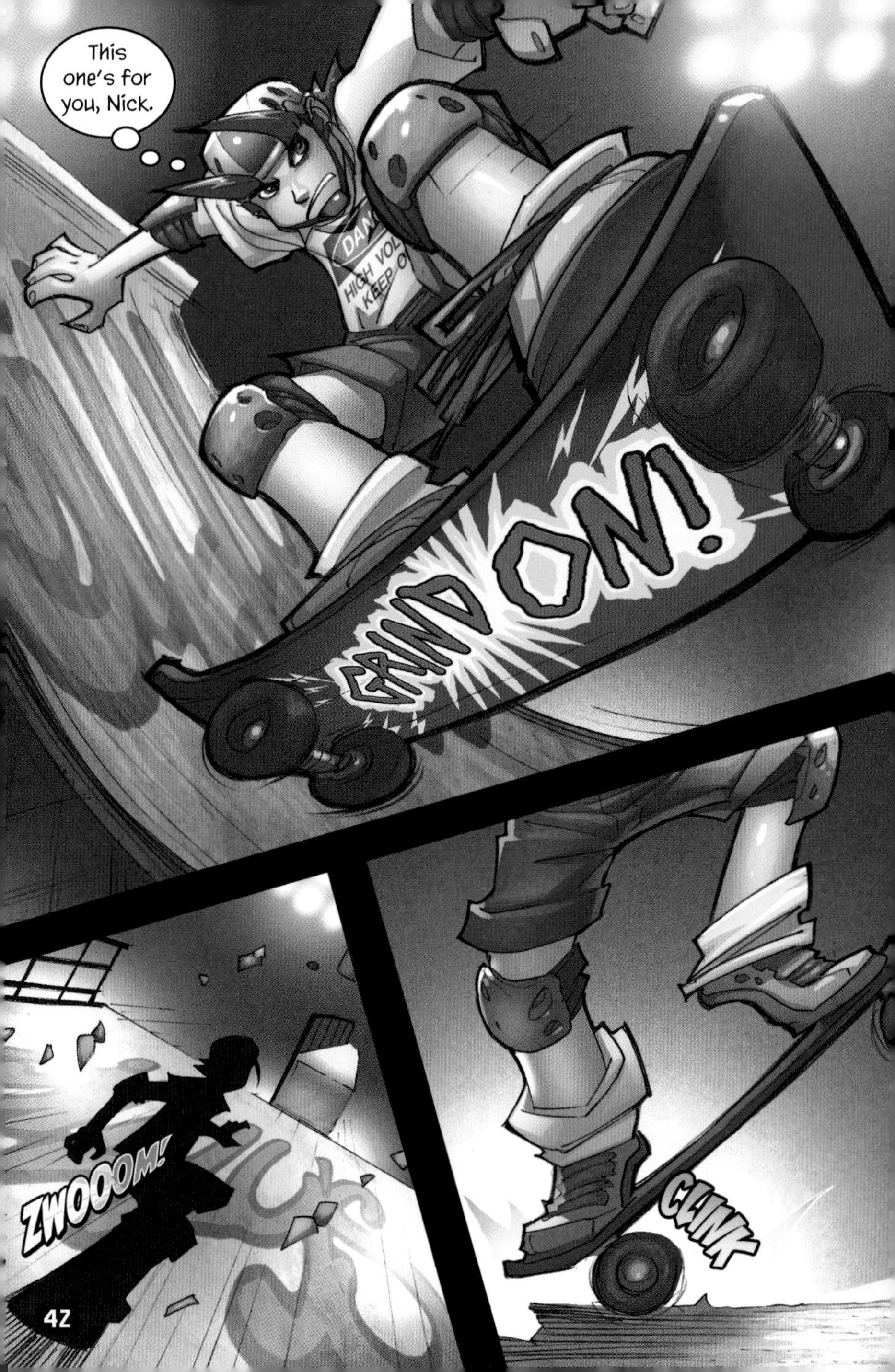
This one's for you, Nick.
GRIND ON!
ZWOOOM!
CLINK

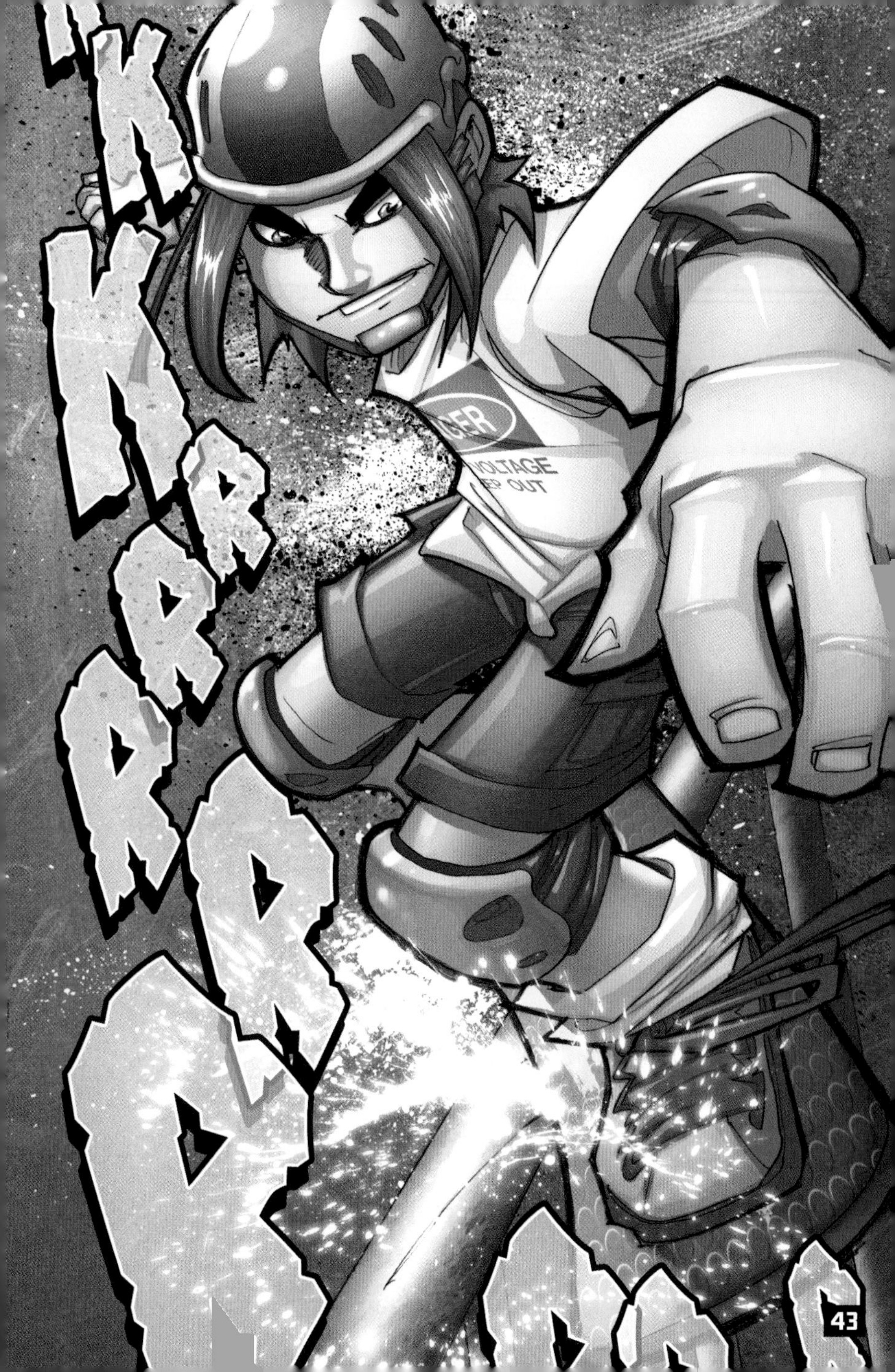
VOLTAGE

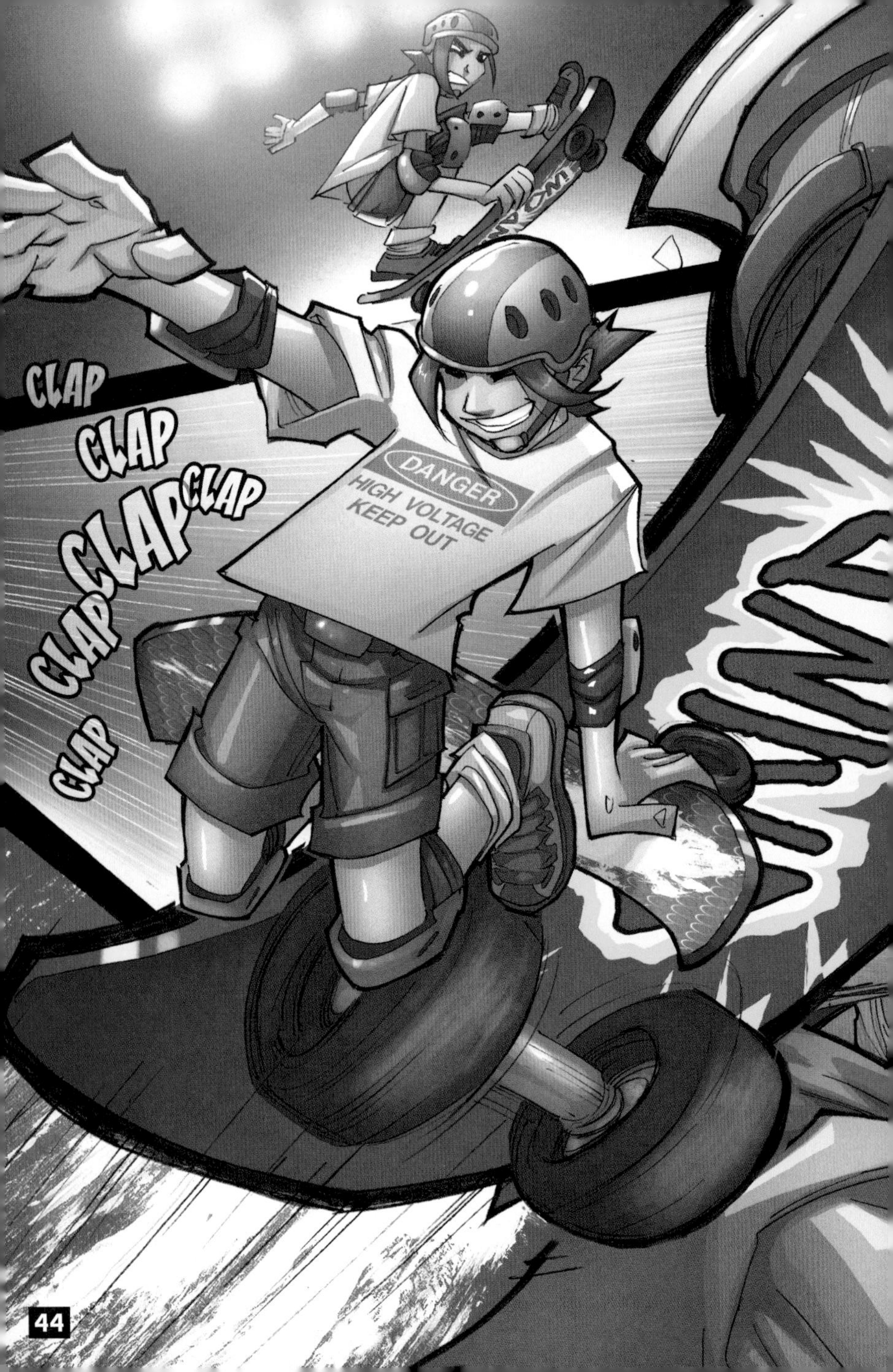
CLAP
CLAP
CLAP
CLAP
CLAP
CLAP
DANGER
HIGH VOLTAGE
KEEP OUT

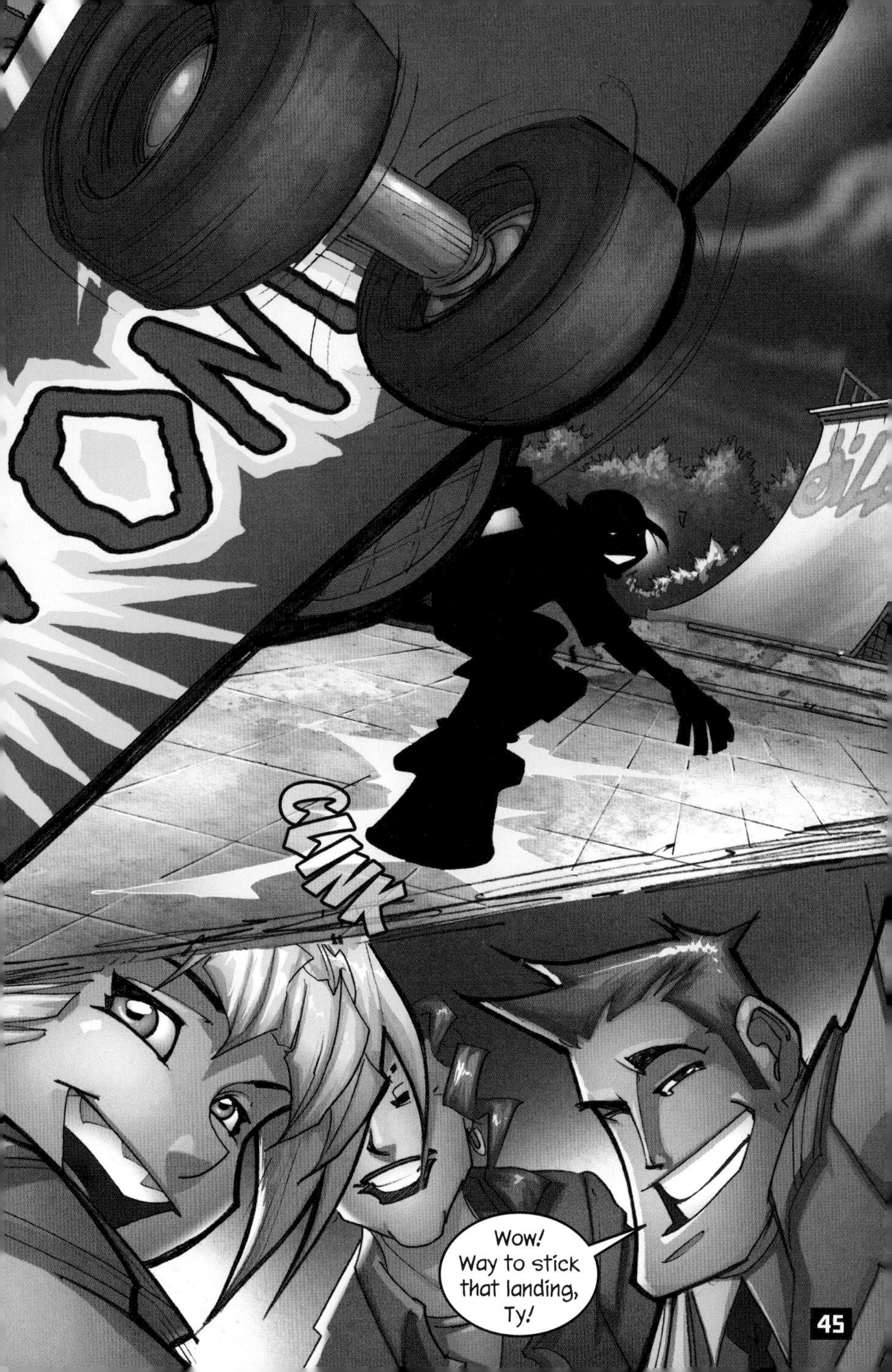
CLINK
Wow! Way to stick that landing, Ty!

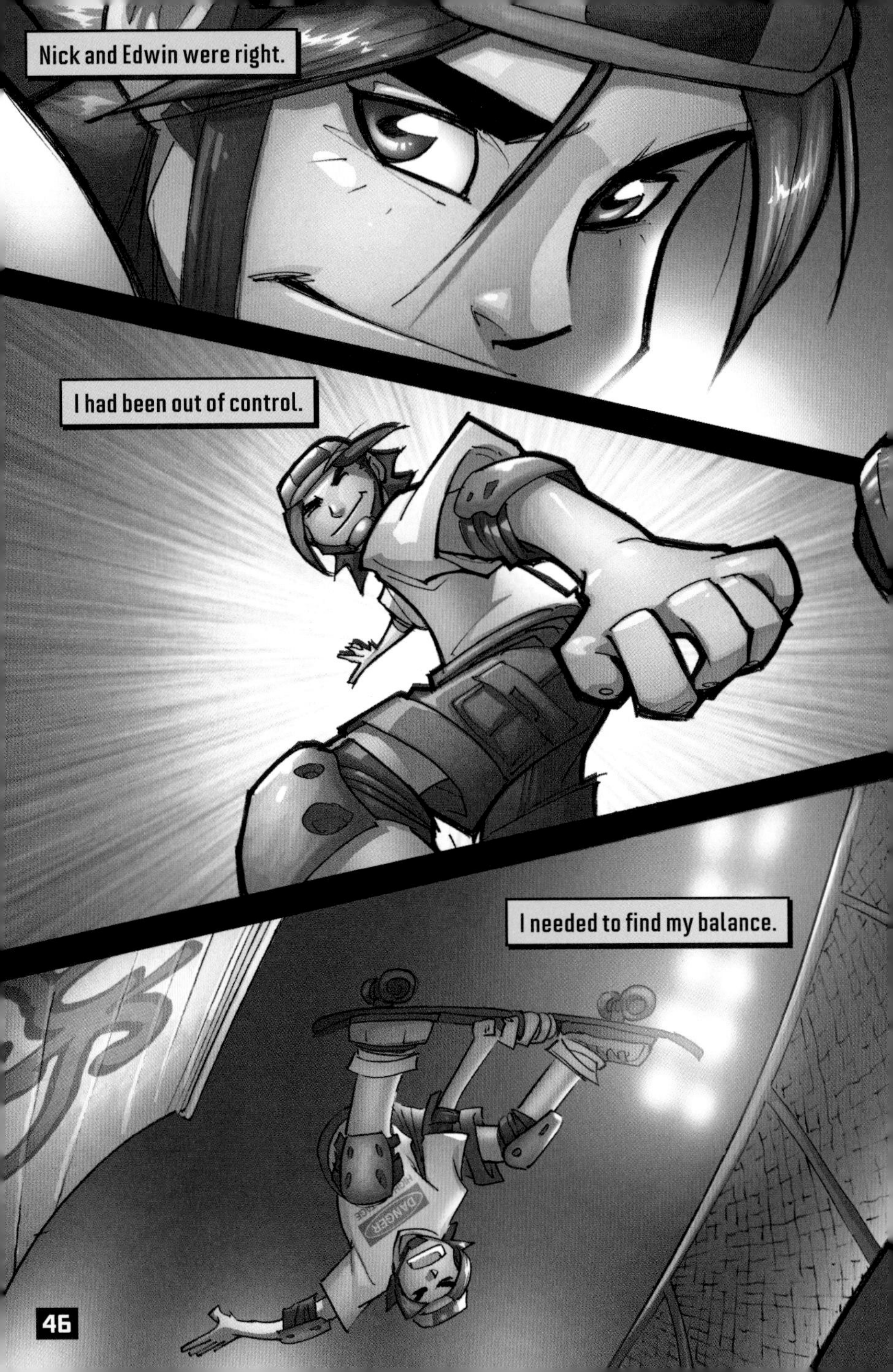
Nick and Edwin were right.
I had been out of control.
I needed to find my balance.
DANGER

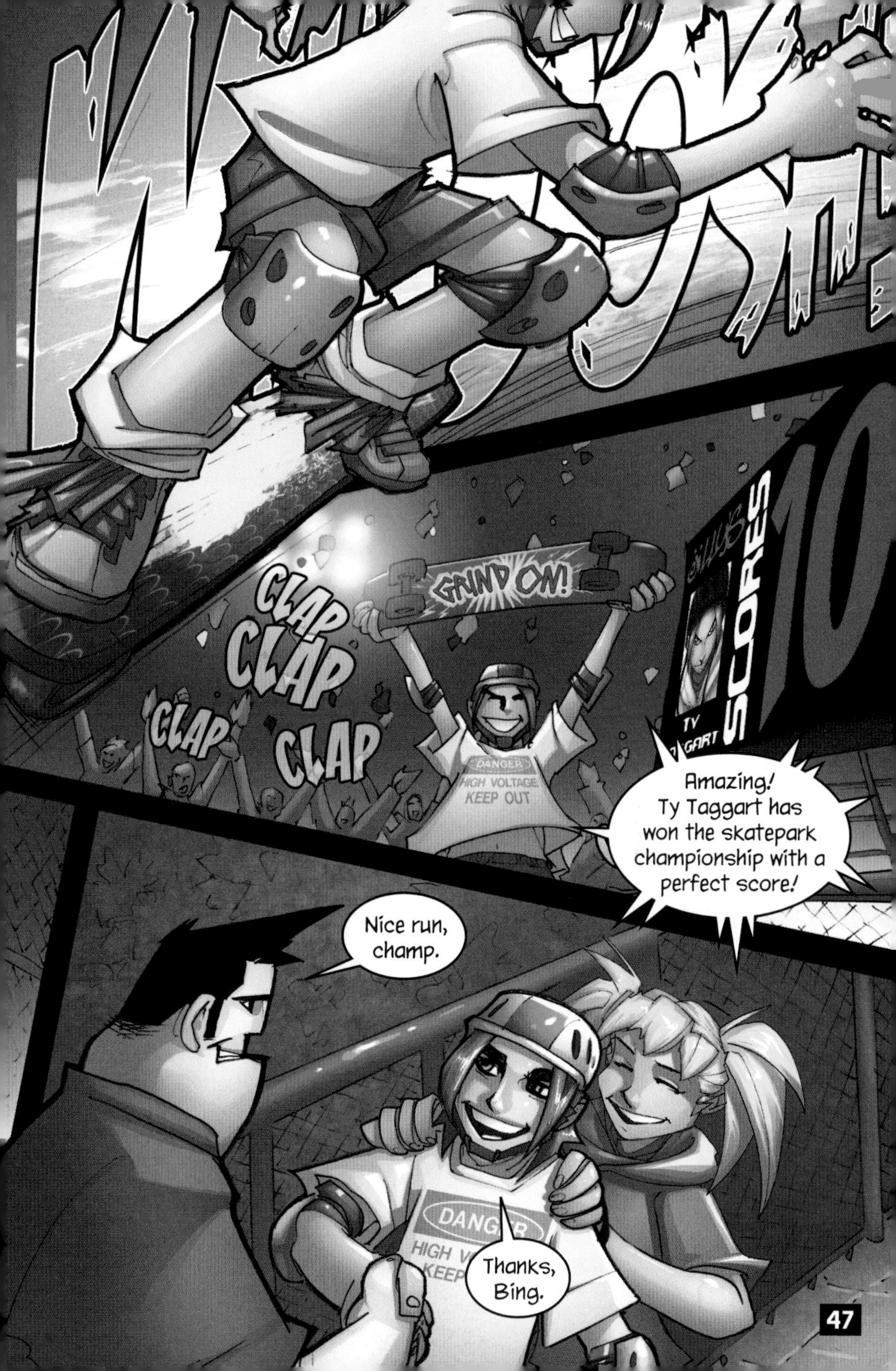
GRIND ON!
CLAP
CLAP
CLAP
CLAP
SCORES
DANGER
HIGH VOLTAGE
KEEP OUT
Amazing! Ty Taggart has won the skatepark championship with a perfect score!
Nice run, champ.
Thanks, Bing.

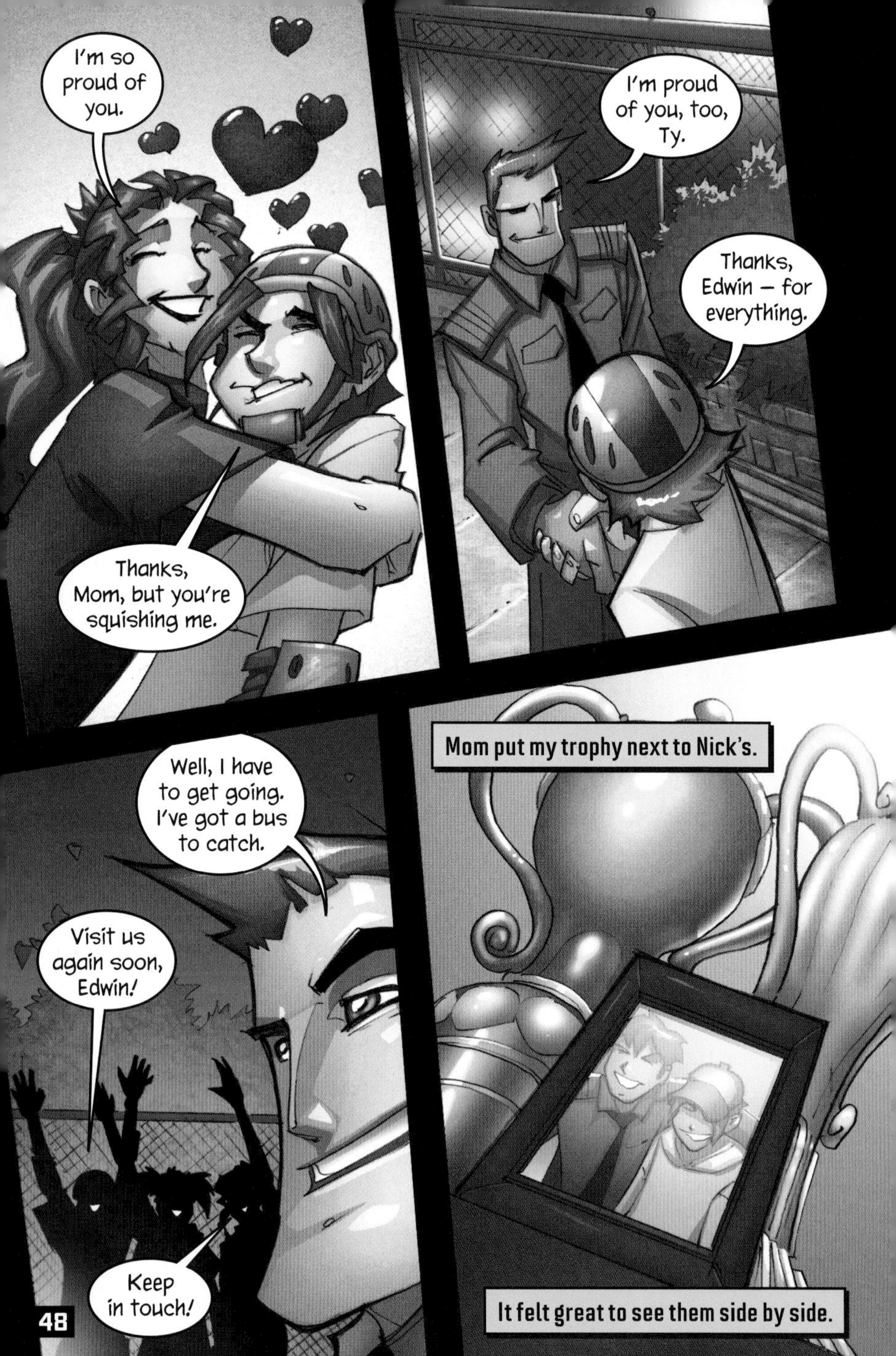
I'm so proud of you.
Thanks, Mom, but you're squishing me.
I'm proud of you, too, Ty.
Thanks, Edwin — for everything.
Well, I have to get going. I've got a bus to catch.
Visit us again soon, Edwin!
Keep in touch!
Mom put my trophy next to Nick's.
It felt great to see them side by side.

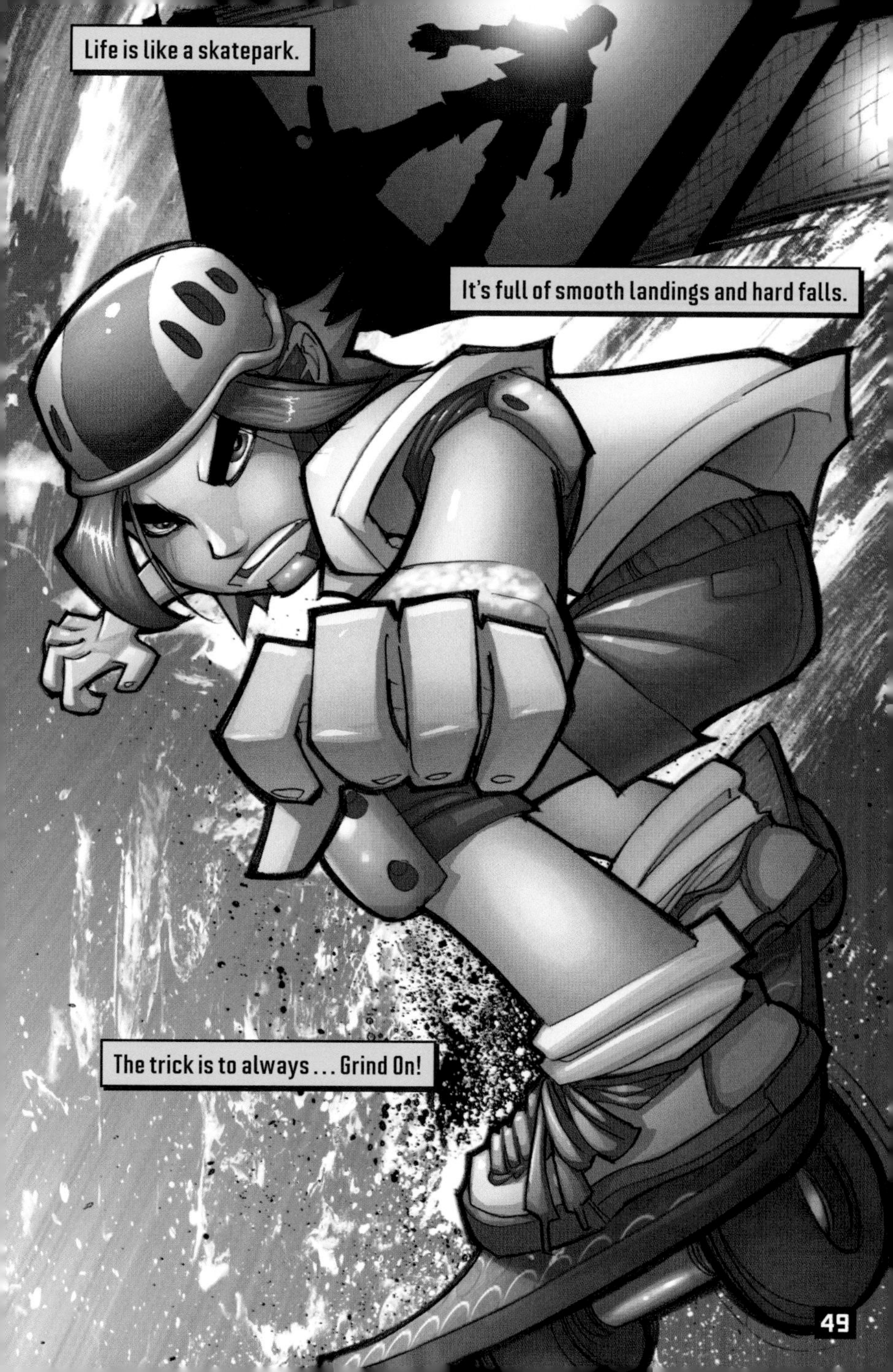
Life is like a skatepark.
It's full of smooth landings and hard falls.
The trick is to always . . . Grind On!

TAGGART

TY TAGGART GRINDS OUT A PERFECT SCORE TO SEAL THE WIN!

BY THE NUMBERS

NAL SCORES:

Y: 10.0
ING: 9.9

STORY: Most people expected Ty Taggart to make a decent showing in this year's championship, but few thought the rising star could outshine white-hot skater Bing Hawtin! Sparks flew as the two stellar teens faced off in the final round ... but once Ty hit his last trick, fans knew there was a new champ in town. Bing Hawtin was quoted as saying, "He may be a little punk, but that Taggart kid sure can grind."

Sports Illustrated KIDS

UP NEXT: *SI KIDS INFO CENTER*

BLZ vs BKS
3-1
TGR vs ROR
33-32
EAG vs BAN
14-7
SPA vs WLD
4-3
BAN vs ROR
21-15
ROR vs LIG
4-3
BLZ vs BKS
3-1

SZ POSTGAME EXTRA

WHERE **YOU** ANALYZE THE GAME!

Skateboarding fans got a real treat today when Ty Taggart one-upped last year's champ, Bing Hawtin, in an amazing skating showdown! Let's go into the stands and ask some fans for their opinions on the day's events...

DISCUSSION QUESTION 1

Ty wins the skating competition. Have you ever won any competitions? What have you done that you're proud of? Talk about it.

DISCUSSION QUESTION 2

Ty Taggart pulls off tons of tricks in this book. What is your favorite skateboarding trick? Describe it.

WRITING PROMPT 1

Edwin helps Ty during a difficult time in his life. Has anyone lent you a hand when you were feeling down? Write about your helpful experience.

WRITING PROMPT 2

Ty's best friend is Jenny Stein. Who is your best friend? Why are the two of you close? What experiences have you had together? Write about your friendship.

(THREE-siks-tee)—a trick that involves spinning three hundred and sixty degrees — or a full rotation — in midair

(AK-suhl)—metal rods that the wheels are connected to

(uh-GRESS-iv)—forceful and fierce

(kri-TEEKD)—pointed out the good and bad parts

(DEK)—the flat surface of a skateboard

(GRIP TAYP)—sandpaper that's placed on the top of the deck. Grip tape provides traction so your feet don't slip.

(KIK-flip)—a trick where the skater kicks the nose of the board up off the ground and into a barrel roll, then lands back on it

(REK-liss)—careless about safety

(TRUHK)—the front and rear axles of a skateboard. The truck connects the wheels to the deck and provides the turning capabilities for the board.

EATORS

ERIC FEIN › *Author*

Eric Fein is a freelance writer and editor. He has edited books for Marvel and DC Comics, which included well-known characters such as Batman, Superman, Wonder Woman, and Spider-Man. Fein has also written dozens of graphic novels and educational children's books.

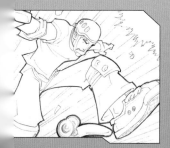

GERARDO SANDOVAL › *Illustrator*

Gerardo Sandoval is a professional comic book illustrator from Mexico. He has worked on many well-known comics, including Tomb Raider books from Top Cow Productions. He has also worked on designs for posters and card sets.

BENNY FUENTES › *Colorist*

Benny Fuentes lives in Villahermosa, Tabasco in Mexico, where it's just as hot as the sauce is. He studied graphic design in college, but now he works as a full-time colorist in the comic book industry for companies like Marvel, DC Comics, and Top Cow Productions. He shares his home with two crazy cats, Chelo and Kitty, who act like they own the place.

Illustrated KIDS GRAPHIC NOVELS

QUICK COMIC

BING HAWTIN, TY TAGGART, and MATTY LYONS IN:

SKATEBOARD SONAR

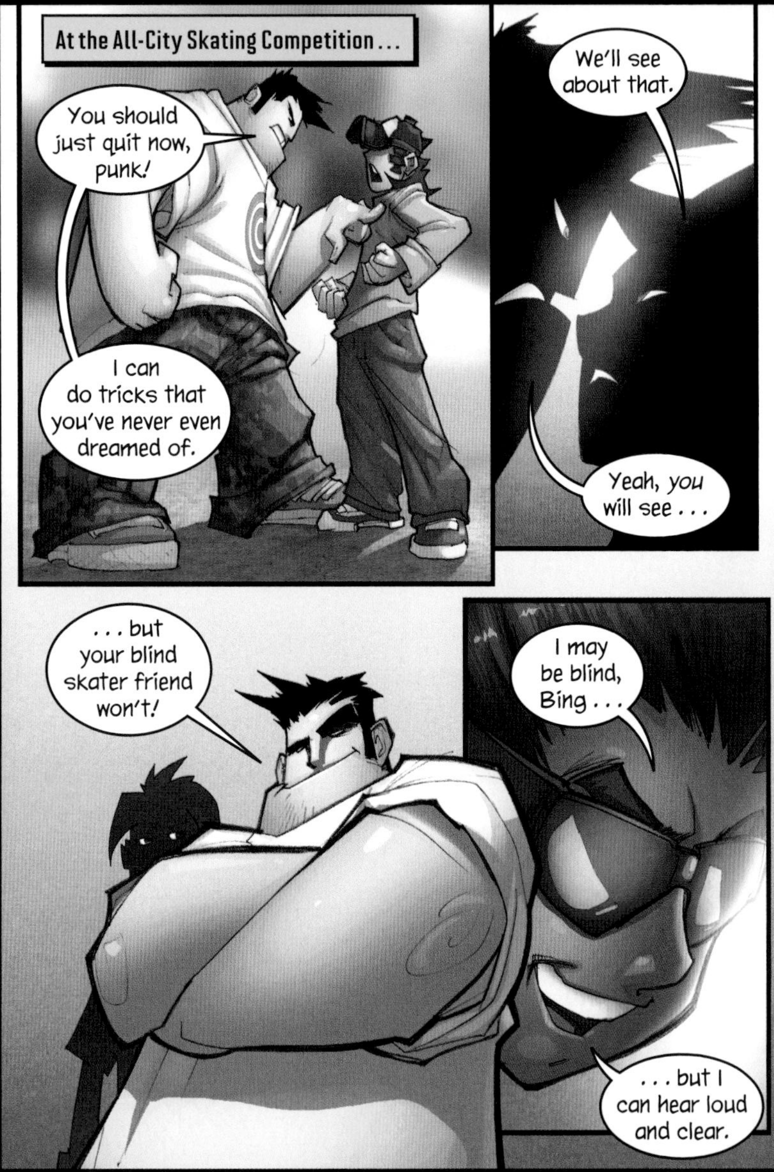

At the All-City Skating Competition . . .
You should just quit now, punk!
I can do tricks that you've never even dreamed of.
We'll see about that.
Yeah, you will see . . .
. . . but your blind skater friend won't!
I may be blind, Bing . . .
. . . but I can hear loud and clear.

» LOVE THIS QUICK COMIC? READ THE WHOLE STORY IN

HOT SPORTS. HOT FORMAT!

GREAT CHARACTERS BATTLE FOR SPORTS GLORY IN TODAY'S HOTTEST FORMAT—GRAPHIC NOVELS!

ONLY FROM **STONE ARCH BOOKS**

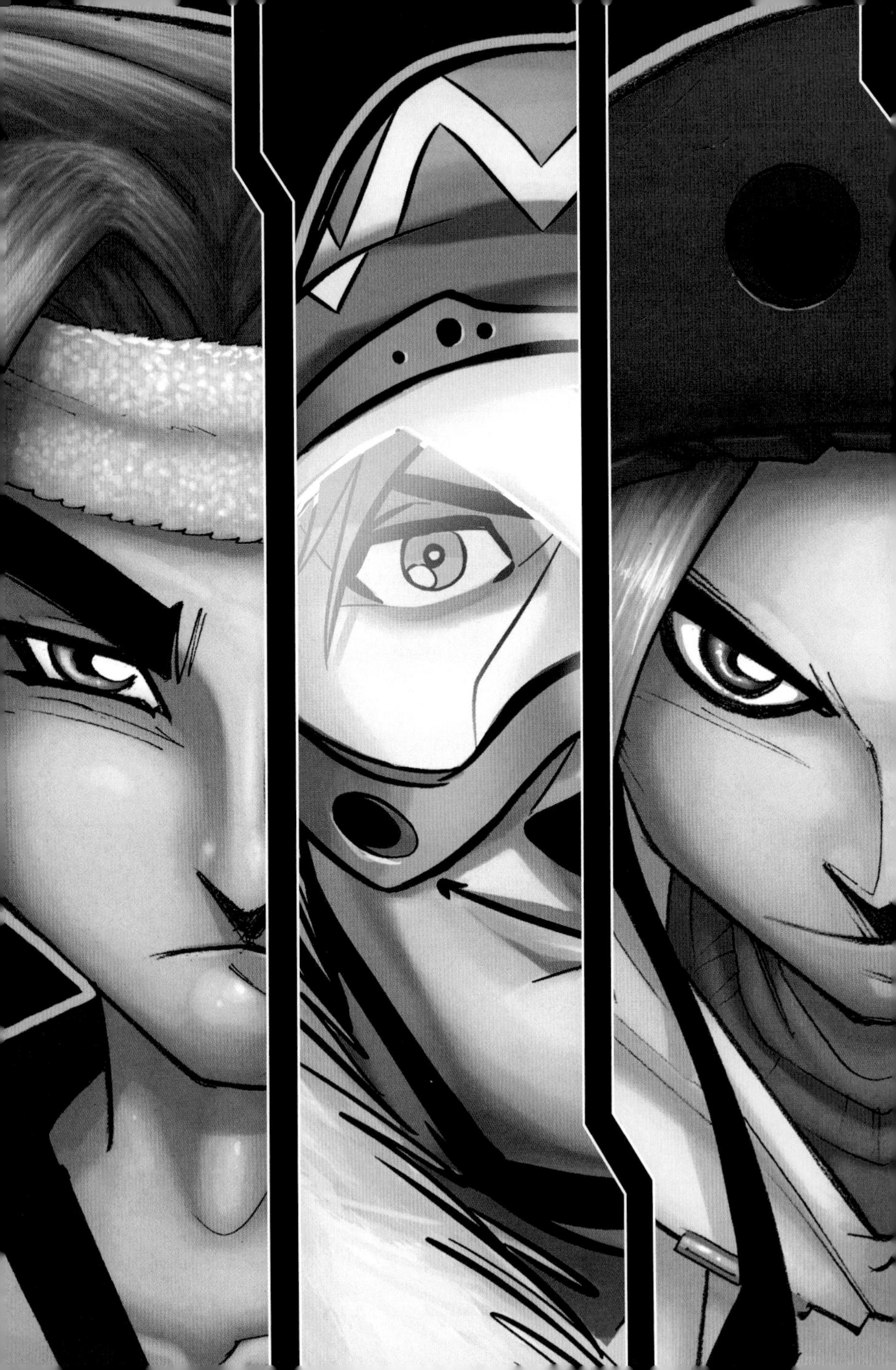

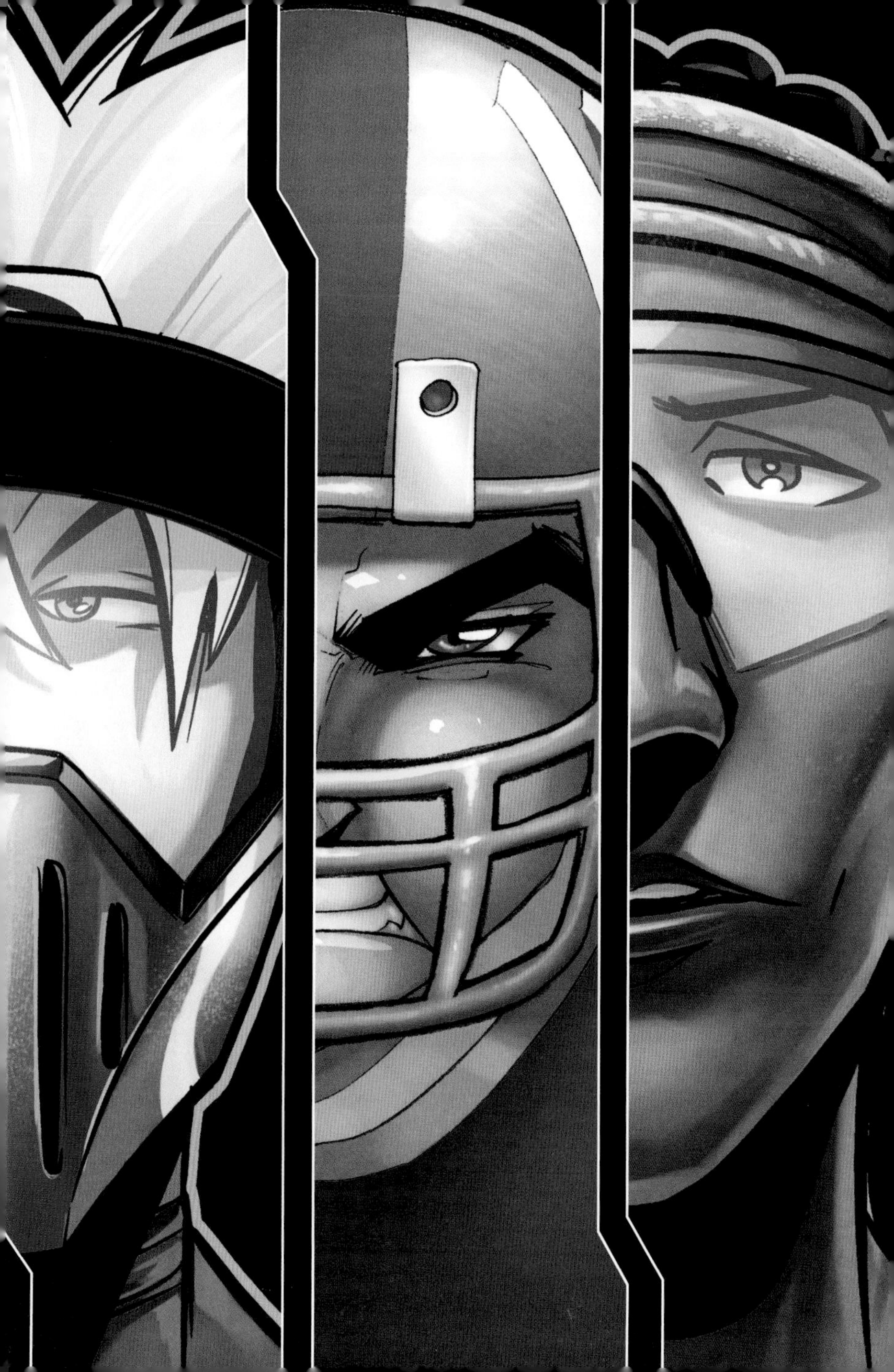

Sports Illustrated KIDS

GRAPHIC NOVELS

STONE ARCH BOOKS
a capstone imprint